Kuska House

The White Princess

MÁRIA ĎURÍČKOVÁ

The White Princess

Illustrated by Miroslav Cipár

KUSKA HOUSE

Kingston, Ontario

Illustrated by Miroslav Cipár
Translated by Heather Trebatická
Graphic design Ján Švec

This edition © KUSKA HOUSE 1988
This illustrated edition first published in 1973 by Mladé letá,
Bratislava, Czechoslovakia
Text © Kuska House 1988

Printed in Czechoslovakia

ISBN 0 920602 02 X

Contents

The White Princess

In a country far away, in the midst of the mountains, there once was a village, and at the very edge of that village, there lived a poor couple with their two sons. The first had already grown into a fine young man, but the second was still a little fellow who couldn't even cut his own bread.

One day, the elder son told his parents that he was leaving home — he wanted to get to know the world and put himself to the test. What could his poor parents do but to let him have his way. His mother baked him some oatcakes, filled a knapsack with food and saw him off into the world.

The young man strode off downhill, the way the water flows, but he had hardly got to the edge of the village when the path suddenly twisted away in the direction of the hills. The young man took the path as he was curious about how people lived on the plain, but very soon he was led once more towards the thick forest. So it happened a third time. In the end, the young man gave up and decided to follow the path wherever it might lead. It led him straight into the deep, black forest.

On and on he went, further and further, deeper and deeper into the forest, until, as dusk was falling, he came to a lonely log hut that was leaning to one side and all covered with moss. As he was tired and night was approaching, he went into the hut.

"A good evening to you," he said politely.

There was no one in the hut but an old woman, with hair as white as milk and a face deeply furrowed with wrinkles. The young man had never seen such an old face in all his life. The old woman was sitting at a table busily writing in a thick book. She gave him neither a glance nor an answer to his greeting.

"I wish you a good evening," he repeated in a louder voice,

thinking that she had probably not heard him the first time. But she said nothing and continued to write, her quill-pen scratching over the paper.

The young man shrugged, slipped his knapsack off his shoulders, sat down on a bench and ate what his mother had prepared for him. Then he stretched himself out, his bag under his head, and before you could count up to five, he was fast asleep.

It was only when he awoke in the morning that the old woman spoke to him. "It was ill fate that brought you here, young lad. I didn't answer your greeting yesterday in the hope that you would go on your way, while there was still time. But you did not leave and so you, too, have become part of our misfortune."

"What misfortune is that? Tell me. Who knows, maybe I can help you."

"Somewhere in this forest there is a well," the old woman began to explain. "If a young man draws water from it without touching the logs that surround it and then I wash in that water, we shall both be happy, and so will a lot of other people. But it is no easy task."

"Easy or not, I shall have a try," declared the young man. "If I have to, I can handle a wolf or a bear, or even a dragon perhaps. I've a good crossbow and a good aim, too."

"That's just it, young man. Nothing will stand in your way: no wolf, no bear, nor any other animal. What you must overcome is far easier, and yet far more difficult. Many a young man has tried to carry out this task, but not one of them has succeeded."

"Come what may, I'll try it," said the young man. "Just tell me how to get to that well, because as I can see, there are a lot of things you know and a lot of things you understand."

"Well, I'll tell you then, although I don't know if it will be of any use to you. On the way to that well, you must go through one, through two and past three."

"Through one what, through two what and past three what?" asked the young man in surprise.

"Through one dark, through two bright and past three dead. But that is all I am allowed to tell you, not a word more," said the old woman and once more returned to her writing.

The lad shook his head in mystification, because these words really

10

had not told him much, but nevertheless he set out. As he was going through the forest, he thought hard what that dark thing could be — a thicket or a cave, or perhaps a chasm? The bright thing could be the flames of a fire. Or perhaps it would be a clearing in the bright sunshine? Or what about the light of the moon?

When the sun shone high above his head, he ate something from his knapsack, drank from a spring and continued his journey. The bright daylight gradually faded and darkness fell. The young man heaped up a pile of dry leaves and lay down in the bed of a dried-up river. He slept well because the bank hung over him like the roof of an old cottage.

In the morning, as dawn was breaking, he set off once more on his venture. He went on and on, but he could see nothing dark, nothing

bright and nothing dead. By lunch time, he developed an appetite for fried bacon. A dry yew stood nearby, so he broke off a branch, made a fire and fried some bacon over it. When he had eaten his fill, he took a drink from a well. The water had a wonderful taste, as sweet as honey. On he went again, keeping a sharp lookout for something dark, something bright and something dead. He mustn't miss them! It was getting for on evening and the sun had already hidden itself behind the tree tops, when he came to a well, beside which there lay the skull of a horse. "What a pity it isn't the well I'm looking for," he thought, "but I can, at least, quench my thirst." He bent over the water and, in doing so, he touched the logs that surrounded the well. No sooner had he touched them, than he turned into a stone.

At home, his parents waited and waited for their son to return and when he didn't come, they thought that either he had met with some misfortune or he was getting on so well in the world that he had completely forgotten about his poor parents. As a result, they showered all their affection on their younger son, Johnny, who by that time had almost grown into a young man.

Then one day, without any warning, their son announced that he was already strong enough and that he, too, would go out into the world; at least he would learn something about life and look for his lost brother. His parents tried their best to persuade him not to go, because if something should happen to him, they were sure to die of sorrow. But his mind was made up, so his mother baked him some oatcakes, filled a knapsack with all kinds of food and, with tears in her eyes, saw him off into the world.

The young man strode off downhill, the way the water flows, but exactly the same thing happened to him as to his brother: the path suddenly twisted away in the direction of the hills, until in the end, it led him to that same lonely log hut.

"A good evening to you," he greeted the old woman who was sitting at the table, writing something in a thick book. But she took no notice of him.

Johnny greeted her a second time, but when she said nothing, he took off his knapsack, ate his supper, stretched out on the bench and fell fast asleep.

In the morning, the old woman said to him, "It was ill fate that

12

brought you to my hut, young man, nothing good awaits you here. When I didn't answer your greeting yesterday, you should have turned around and gone away. Now it is too late and you, too, have become part of our misfortune."

"What misfortune is that? I have a good crossbow and I'm daring enough, maybe I can help you."

"Maybe you can," replied the old woman thoughtfully. She told him all about the well and how the way to it led through one dark, two bright and past three dead. He must draw water from the well without touching the logs that surrounded it.

Johnny set out into the forest. As he went along, he thought hard what that dark, bright and dead could be. When the night was approaching like a dark, robed woman from the other side of the forest, an idea suddenly struck him: the bright something must be the day and the dark the night, which meant the journey would take two days and one night.

13

Johnny prepared a bed for himself under the same bank of the dried-up river as his brother had before. "Shelter me under your bank, dear dead river," he said and without a word, the dead river gave him shelter, its bank offering him a roof over his head.

"This is the first dead thing I have to pass," Johnny thought to himself.

Early in the morning, he set off again and did not stop before noon, when he felt an appetite for fried bacon. He looked around him and caught sight of a dry yew tree.

"Give me a branch or two, dear dead yew," said Johnny, breaking off a branch and building a fire. This is the second dead thing I have to pass, he thought. He ate his fill and went on his way.

On and on he went until it was almost dusk, when he suddenly came to a clearing where he saw a well and a white, parched horse skull lying nearby.

"Help me to draw water, dear dead horse," he said as he stepped up to the well. Taking great care not to touch the logs that surrounded it, he bent over the well. He had hardly touched the surface of the water when he heard a whinnying and prancing of hoofs. There beside him stood a fairy horse. "Lose no time now, draw some water and jump up on my back."

Johnny looked around and his eye fell on a little jug lying beside the spring. He filled it with water, leapt astride the fairy horse and flew back to the log hut. The journey which had taken him two days before was now covered in the blink of an eye.

In front of the log hut, the horse neighed and the old woman appeared in the doorway and stretched out her arms.

Johnny handed her the jug of water. She poured some into her

14

palm and washed her face with it. At that moment, three flashes of lightning pierced the sky. When Johnny had collected his wits, he saw, instead of the old woman, a beautiful princess all in white with a star shining in her hair. Where the hut had stood, there was now a palace and the thick forest had become a beautiful city. People streamed out of the houses, thanking him for setting them free and bowing to the love-ly White Princess. Knights and young men, each differently dressed and armed, be-gan to arrive. Men who had been changed into stones beside the spring. All of them re-joicing in their regai-ned freedom. In front of the crowd, there strode a man who was Johny's own elder brother.

Soon afterwards, a wedding took place. A grandiose, royal wed-ding: the White Prin-cess was marrying her rescuer. John's parents were invited to the wedding and they could not get over their happiness at seeing both of their lost sons.

After three days of feasting and dancing, the guests were exhausted. John gave a sign to the musicians to stop playing and he addressed his wife: "Dear White Princess, now tell us what you know and what is still a mystery to us. How it all happened, up to the moment when it was all put right again."

15

"All thanks to you, Prince John," said the White Princess, bowing to him so deeply that the star in her hair gleamed like the sun. Then she took her place on the stately throne and began: "How pleasant it is to speak about it now that it is all over! But listen. I once had three magic friends. The first was my fairy horse. Whenever an enemy attacked our country, my fairy horse would carry me in a flash to the place where the fighting was going on. When the soldiers saw me flying over the battlefield on my fairy horse, new strength flowed into their veins. In those days there was a song that could be heard throughout the country:

> We have a White Princess,
> Beautiful and wise.
> She rides a magic horse,
> Victory in her eyes.

My second magic friend was the river, Olda. If we were attacked by powerful enemies, Olda would overflow its banks and drown them all. My third magic friend was a tall yew tree. Every year we could make seven bows from that yew — magic bows that never missed their target. That is why our archers were the best and most feared throughout the world. With the help of these three magic friends, our kingdom was so strong that no one could ever defeat us. Thus we lived in peace and happiness.

But one day a large caravan arrived at our court from a far-off country. A thousand camels carrying treasure chests of jewels and precious stones, fine cloth, rich carpets, and golden cages with birds we had never seen before. On the largest camel, under an azure blue canopy, sat the Black King. He had come to ask my hand in marriage and he was sure I would agree, after all he was one of the most powerful kings in the whole world. But I refused him. Not because I did not like the Black King, but because I did not want to leave my country for anything in the world. The Black King took offense and declared war on us. His efforts were in vain because with the help of my three magic friends, we sent his armies fleeing time and time again. Unfortunately, the Black King was skilled in sorcery. From the sand and the wind, he discovered the source of our strength and pronounced a terrible curse: "May this land change into a thick forest, its ruler into an ugly old woman, may the magic river and the magic yew dry up for ever and may magpies and crows tear the fairy horse apart with their beaks!''

That is what happened and was to remain so for ever and a day. Our country grew wild, the centuries flew over it like a flock of birds and the world around gradually forgot about us, until we had fallen into oblivion. Nothing remained of us except the little song:

We have a White Princess,
Beautiful and wise.
She rides a magic horse,
Victory in her eyes.

In the end, it wasn't even a song. Children used to chant it as part of their games so everyone thought it was just a nursery rhyme. It never even occurred to anyone that it could be a reminder of a kingdom and its ruler from times long ago.

All this time I sat in my poor log hut, writing down everything that had happened to us. I made a record of the wisdom of our people, their mistakes and faults, and all the secrets of our land. As I wrote it down, word by word, I began to come to the conclusion that our ill fate would last a long, long time, but that it would not last forever. That sooner or later, a young man would appear who would guess what the one dark, two bright could mean and who would recognize, in the middle of the forest, the three dead things. This young man would bring us back to life. That is how it was: the roads and paths began to twist away in our direction and lead brave young men to us, until at last you arrived. Long live John, may he justly rule this country at my side for many years to come!''

The wedding was brought to an end and the guests departed. John and his beautiful wife lived on in the palace, happy together. From time to time, the White Princess would saddle her fairy horse and fly off to the mountains. One leap would take her to the Matras, another to the Fatras and a third to the Tatras.

Tom Thumb

There was once a country and in that country, a village and in that village, at the very edge, next to the path, there was a cottage. The cottage was neither small nor big, but just the right size for a father, a mother and their seven sons. For a father bent from hard work, for a mother grey with worry, for six sons, as tall and handsome as six poplar trees and for the seventh tiny little boy. The seventh was as tiny as the thumb on your hand, or even tinier: like the thumb of a child too young to go to school.

That is why they named him Tom Thumb.

As usually happens, the mother was fondest of this little boy. No wonder. After all, it was he who clung to her most and kept her amused with his chatter, like a happy little bird.

Tom Thumb used to sleep on the wide stove in a tiny little cradle made out of an eggshell, and loved to rock to and fro. He would lie down in his cradle and sing so loud that the walls would shake:

> *Rock me, cradle, rock*
> *To and fro, to and fro.*
> *When I want to stop,*
> *Let me go, let me go.*

The cradle strained itself so hard to please him that from time to time it would crack. But that did not matter. His mother made his bed up in another eggshell and the room would soon shake again with his song:

> *Rock me, cradle, rock,*
> *To and fro, to and fro!*

Even more than being at home with his mother, Tom Thumb enjoyed the company of his big brothers. He was at the age when boys like most of all to be with men.

Once the brothers went to mow and they took Tom Thumb with

them. They put him down at the edge of the field beside their bundle of bread and set to work. The scythes rang out, the grass rustled and Tom Thumb leaned up against the boundary stone, gazed around him and chattered to the ants. At this moment, a butterfly came fluttering up to him:

"Welcome to the meadow, Tom Thumb!"

"Welcome to you, too," Tom Thumb replied.

"And what are you doing, just sitting here? Wouldn't you like to see the wide world?"

"Yes, I would! I'd love to!"

"Then sit on my back!"

Tom Thumb didn't have to be told twice. He sat astride the butterfly as if it were a fairy horse and off it flew, up into the air. It flew over meadows, over fields, over clover patches, over hills, over valleys, over towering black cliffs. They went a long, long way.

"Look, we are flying over a river!" said the butterfly. Tom Thumb gazed down at that wide stretch of water, something darted around in it. He bent over to get a better look, but he should not have done that. He slipped off the silky back of the butterfly and splash! The water closed over his head.

The thing he had seen darting around in the water had been a greedy pike. It opened its mouth and snap! It had swallowed Tom Thumb like a raspberry.

To his great luck, just at that moment a fisherman was catching fish nearby. When his basket was full, he carried it off to the royal palace, because he was the royal fishmonger.

The royal cook emptied the fish onto the table and began to clean them. He was in a great hurry because he was behind with the lunch. So it happened that when he opened the biggest fish, something live slipped out of it. Not everyone notices a person if he is as tiny as a thumb.

Tom Thumb rubbed his eyes and saw the blade of a knife flashing dangerously near him. Frightened for his life, he took to his heels, clambering over the pile of fish. But the table was not so very big and Tom Thumb, rushing blindly on, plunged into something soft and cold. It smelt of strawberries, it tasted of strawberries. The poor little

boy didn't know what he had fallen into, he had never seen the like of it in his mother's cottage. But we know what it was and we will tell you: Tom Thumb had fallen into the strawberry ice cream. His teeth chattered with cold, but even so, for safety's sake he pushed himself further into the cold dessert. Indeed, it was high time, because the ice cream was just then whisked away to the royal table.

At the royal table sat the royal parents with their daughter, Marietta. The royal parents were just saying in unison, "Princess Marietta, eat up your spinach and we'll give you a new coat."

But Princess Marietta tossed her head, "I don't want a new coat! I want strawberry ice cream!"

The royal parents looked sadly at each other and once again said in unison, "Princess Marietta, help yourself to cabbage and we'll give you a talking doll."

20

But the princess retorted, "I don't want a talking doll! I want strawberry ice cream!"

The royal parents knew that they ought to try to persuade her once more, but they also knew that it would still be in vain. So they just looked at each other sadly and gave their daughter the strawberry ice cream.

Princess Marietta scooped up a large spoonful of ice cream and was just about to put it into her mouth when she suddenly noticed that something was wriggling in it: something small, alive, with two little arms, two little legs, one head and a hat on top of it.

"Well, I never! It's a little boy!" she cried out in delight. "What's your name, little boy?"

The little boy took off his hat, made a sweeping bow and said, "I am Tom Thumb and I wish you good health, achoo!"

"Tom Thumb!" Princess Marietta clapped her hands. She was beside herself with joy. Until that moment, she had always been the smallest person in the palace, and all of a sudden here was someone much, much smaller. He called himself Tom Thumb, had fallen into the ice cream and caught a cold, achoo!

At once she ordered the servants to bring a thimbleful of hot tea from the kitchens. First camomile tea, then linden, rose-hip and jasmine. She wondered what other kinds of tea she should order, but for one thing, there were no more thimbles in the palace and for the other, no more tea was needed, because Tom Thumb had already recovered.

From then on he lived in the royal palace and he was better off than he had ever been before. He slept in a golden bed, ate cakes, ice cream and all kinds of thing he had never seen before and everyone honored him and held him in respect. Not because he was so exceptional, but for the reason that Princess Marietta was fond of him. The princess liked him so much, that she quickly ate her spinach, her cabbage and her carrots too, so that she could play with her dear, little friend.

At first, Tom Thumb enjoyed living in the palace, but not for long. More and more often, he was to be seen with a frown on his face.

"What's the matter with you, Tom Thumb?" asked Princess Marietta.

"What's the matter, what's the matter! I don't even know that myself," grumbled Tom Thumb. "Oh, yes I do! In this palace there is nothing but marble, silver, and gold. Not a meadow, a field, or an ant or a butterfly in sight. That's what the matter is."

"But... but you'd get lost in a meadow!" Princess Marietta was horrified at the thought. "You'd lose your way like in a deep forest. But don't be sad. I'll think of something." She really did.

She summoned a craftsman and ordered him to carve a tiny coach out of wood. Then she had two white mice harnessed to this coach and presented it to Tom Thumb on the very day when he was feeling most sad.

Tom Thumb was very pleased with the coach. He drove up and down the paths in the royal park, enjoying himself among the grass, flowers, ants and butterflies. He looked hard for his butterfly friend who had carried him away from his father's meadow, but he was nowhere to be seen. That made Tom Thumb very sad.

"What's the matter with you now, Tom Thumb?" asked Princess Marietta.

"What's the matter, what's the matter! I don't even know that myself," grumbled Tom. "Oh yes, I do! I'm missing my six brothers, my mother and my father."

"If that's all!" Princess Marietta threw up her arms in relief. "That can be put right. We'll send our minister for them."

The king and queen were quite ready to agree to Princess

Marietta's suggestion. They called for the minister and he asked, "Well, where do your parents live, Tom Thumb?"

"In our village, right beside the path," said Tom Thumb. "They have a cottage with a garden and rosemary in the window."

The minister set out to look for Tom Thumb's parents. He travelled here and there, forever losing his way and came back with empty hands.

"I've gone through three hundred villages and looked into three thousand cottages with gardens and rosemary in the windows. But your parents don't live in any of them."

Tom Thumb hung his head sadly.

"Don't worry, dear Tom, I'll think of something," Princess Marietta comforted him.

They had in their park a big bird called Perdix. Marietta hung a tiny basket around Perdix's neck, put Tom Thumb in the basket and told him, "Go home and tell your brothers and parents to come and live in the royal town. Tell them, it is a message from the king himself."

Perdix spread his wings and flew off, going in whichever direction Tom Thumb pointed. Very soon they were in the village where, just beside the path, stood the cottage in which Tom had been born.

What rejoicing there was when the little boy appeared so unexpectedly in the doorway, calling out, "Good health to you, father, mother and to you my brothers!" They threw their arms round him, kissing him and gazing in wonder at his royal clothes and the gold feather in his cap. When they had gazed their fill, Tom Thumb asked them whether they would go back with him to live in the royal town.

"I wouldn't say no," said his

father, "but only if they build us a cottage there just like the one we have here."

"If they give us fields and cattle," said his brothers.

"And if they give us a yard with a henhouse, so that I can raise hens," said his mother. "You know how many eggshells are needed for your cradle."

Tom Thumb told them that Princess Marietta was sure to give them all they wanted and so they agreed to move.

The king had a cottage built for them, just like the one they were used to, and beside it was a garden and a yard with a henhouse, just like the one at home, and he gave them fields and cattle. They were happy and contented.

But even happier was Princess Marietta. Her friend was always near at hand and she could play with him as much as she liked.

But happiest of all was Tom Thumb: when he wanted, he could play with Princess Marietta, when he wanted, he could ride around in his coach pulled by mice, and when he wanted, he could go out into the fields with his big brothers. In the evening, he lay down in his egg-shell cradle, rocked himself to and fro and sang till the walls all shook,

> *Rock me, cradle, rock,*
> *To and fro, to and fro,*
> *When I want to stop,*
> *Let me go, let me go!*

But that was all a long, long time ago. Not even my mother remembers this, she, too, only heard the tale from others.

The Bridegroom from the Well

It wasn't far, it wasn't near, it wasn't there, it wasn't here. In a little village in the hills, there lived a mother with her three daughters. They were shapely girls and their mother lived only for them, she saw herself reflected in them like the sky in a lake. But not only her eyes were drawn to them. Young men turned their heads to gaze whenever they passed by. Especially if it was the youngest, Dora she was called, because she was the loveliest of them all.

They lived simple but happy lives, until one day their mother fell ill. She grew so weak, they feared she was dying. Her daughters almost went out of their minds with worry and ran about the village in search of herbs and good advice.

"I know what would help your mother," one old woman told them. "In the middle of the river, two days' journey upstream from the footbridge, is an islet and on that islet, a magic well. If your mother drinks water from that well, she will recover completely."

No sooner had the girls heard this than they decided to bring her water from that well. The eldest of them set out. She waded across the river, let her bucket down into the well and drew water. But there was a crayfish swimming in the bucket. He waved his pincers and said,

> *Water you can draw,*
> *Water of life,*
> *If only you promise*
> *To become my wife.*

The girl stared at him in horror. "I, the wife of a repulsive, whiskery creature like you?!" she cried out. "I'd sooner never marry at all!" She threw the bucket back into the well and ran off home.

"Have you got it?" asked her sisters anxiously.

"No, I haven't. The rope broke and the bucket fell into the well."

The middle sister hurried off to fetch the water. She waded across the river and drew a bucketful of water and there was the black crayfish. It waved its tail and said,

> *Water you can draw,*
> *Water of life,*
> *If only you promise*
> *To become my wife.*

"I, the wife of an ugly creature with claws like you?!" the girl shivered with repulsion. "I'd sooner never marry anyone!" She threw the bucket into the well and ran off home.

"Well, have you got it?" the youngest sister ran out to meet her, for their mother was losing strength fast.

"No, I haven't. The bucket fell into the well," the middle sister said, her eyes cast down in shame.

The youngest daughter hurried off to bring the water. She waded across the river, pulled up a full bucket and there was the black crayfish, waving its claws and tail and saying.

> *Water you can draw,*
> *Water of life,*
> *If only you promise*
> *To become my wife.*

"Not for anything in the world!" Dora thought to herself. But then she remembered her mother, more dead than alive, and she was seized by fear for her, so she answered quickly, "Very well, I'll be your wife." She drew water and hurried home as fast as her legs would carry her.

The water had hardly touched her mother's lips when she immediately recovered and rose from her bed.

The cottage was once more filled with happiness and joyful laughter. But not for long.

No sooner had it grown dark, than they heard a voice outside the door:

> *Water you drew,*
> *Water of life.*
> *But Dora, you promised*
> *To become my wife.*

Dora froze in horror. But what could she do, a promise is

26

a promise, so she opened the door and waited until her crayfish bridegroom had sidled in. He came to a halt in the middle of the room.

"How handsomely your bridegroom shuffles along!" giggled the eldest sister.

"That ugly creature is to be our brother-in-law?" the middle sister gave him such a kick that the crayfish was thrown onto its back with its legs waving helplessly in the air.

Dora suddenly felt sorry for the crayfish. She picked him up and placed him on the bench.

The time came for supper. When the food was on the table, the crayfish spoke up,

> *Put me on the table,*
> *My future wife,*
> *A promise you exchanged*
> *For water of life.*

"Whatever next!" exclaimed the eldest sister. "You're not going to let that creature eat with us from one dish! Take this poker and whack him over the head!" She handed the poker to Dora.

Dora would have been quite glad to get rid of her repulsive

bridegroom, but she could not forget how he had helped her and what she had promised in return. So she put the poker away in the corner, lifted the crayfish from the bench and put him on the table.

When supper was over, the mother and her daughters got ready for bed. The youngest brought a little blanket to make a bed for the crayfish, but he spoke out once more,

> *Put me in your bed,*
> *My future wife,*
> *A promise you exchanged*
> *For water of life.*

Both the older girls broke into fits of giggles and Dora's eyes filled with tears of shame. But what could she do? A promise is a promise. She put the crayfish in her bed and lay down beside him. She wet the pillow with tears until midnight came.

On the stroke of midnight there came a terrible rumble-tumble, boom and crash, the ceiling cracked, the roof fell in, as if the world was coming to an end. When the first light of dawn came through the windows, they saw in the bed not a crayfish, but a handsome prince. The room was no longer a room, but a beautiful chamber. The cottage not a cottage, but a splendid palace with four towers, forty halls and four hundred windows.

The prince knelt in front of Dora and said to her,

> *You kept your word*
> *And set me free.*
> *Now be my bride*
> *And marry me.*

Very soon there was a wedding and what a wedding! The prince invited not only the whole village, but the whole country. They ate, drank, feasted, sang and danced. The fields sang too, the forest danced, that wedding is remembered to this very day. Only two people were not there, the young bride's sisters. One of them had turned quite green with envy and the other quite yellow, so they were ashamed to show themselves in public.

The Ploughman and the Giant

Once a farmer was ploughing his little field at the foot of the mountains. He was walking behind his oxen, cracking his whip and glancing around from time to time. Suddenly, he noticed a woman striding down the slope, an enormous woman, a giantess. She was coming straight towards him. His first thought was to run away and hide behind the nearest bush. But what would become of the oxen? An ox won't turn and run, any fool knows that, and what farmer would abandon his beasts in time of danger? So he stayed where he was, leaving his fate to fortune.

Meanwhile, the giantess had caught up with him. She bent over and stared at him with eyes as large as moons. Suddenly, she broke into laughter and clapped her huge hands in delight. Then she knelt down and, spreading her apron over her knees, picked up the ploughman together with his oxen and plough and off she strode back to the mountains, laughing and skipping along in joy.

"Could she be going to eat me up together with the oxen?" the ploughman shivered in fear. He peered out of the apron, trying to see where the giantess was taking him.

Meanwhile, she had reached the highest peak. The ploughman saw that running between the cliffs were beautiful, smooth roads with splendid gates leading off them. These gates didn't lead to houses, but straight into the cliffs. The giantess turned off through one gate, put the ploughman and his oxen down on a huge stone table and ran out, crying, "Look what I have found!"

The ploughman looked round to see where he was: a vast chamber with red, green and blue gems studding the walls and lighting up the chamber like large lamps. Standing on the floor there was an enormous bed and stools covered with bear skins. On the table a knife, as long as a sword, next to it a loaf of bread. "What a loaf!"

29

thought the ploughman. "If they ate the middle out of it, my house and yard would fit inside the crust."

Before he could take everything in, a crowd of giants rushed into the room. They shouted, exclaimed and laughed a deafening din. They pressed around the tables, picking up the ploughman and his oxen and passing them from palm to palm. "For heavens' sake," he thought, closing his eyes tightly, "if they drop me, that'll be the end of me."

"Did your father bring you that, Suzy?" one giant asked.

"Oh no!" the giantess answered proudly, "I found it all by myself, down at the foot of the mountains."

"What was he doing there?"

"He was just amusing himself, walking up and down the field with these tiny creatures with horns," giggled Suzy.

This was more than the ploughman could bear. "I was ploughing, if you want to know, and that's no game!" he shouted at the top of his voice.

The giants stopped talking and gazed at him in astonishment. It was a moment before Suzy asked, "What is 'ploughing'?"

"It's real hard work," said the ploughman. "If no one ploughed, there would be no grain and no bread."

At that moment, the door opened and another giant stepped in, and he was at least twice as big as the others. Suzy ran up to him and cried, "Daddy, daddy, look what I've got! I found him on the field at the foot of the mountains."

The father looked down at the table and said, "Welcome among us, little man!"

The ploughman lifted his hat, "The best of health to you, Mr. Giant."

The giant took his daughter's hand and said to her, "Suzy, take this man and his oxen back where you found him and let him get on with his work."

Then he sat down at the table and addressed the ploughman. "Please excuse my daughter, little man, she's still a child and doesn't know very much about the world. I'm very sorry. Her ignorance must have caused you considerable fear. Tell me what I can give you in return."

"There's no need for that," said the ploughman, "after all, I'm safe and sound. But if you would really like to do something for me, cut a slice off your bread and give it to me, so that people down there can see the bread that giants eat."

The giant cut off a slice of bread and placed it in a basket alongside the ploughman and his oxen. Suzy carried the basket to the field and

put the ploughman back, exactly at the spot where he had left off ploughing.

"What else can I do for you?" she asked.

"Be so kind and put the slice of bread on that cart I use to carry my plough."

Suzy put the slice on the cart and then strode off without a word, four or five strides taking her to the top of the mountain slope, where she disappeared among the rocks.

The ploughman finished ploughing his field and, as dusk was falling, he returned home with his cart. As he went along, people stopped him at every house, all wanting to know about the gigantic slice.

"That is a slice of bread from the land of giants," said the ploughman proudly. "Cut a bit off and taste the bread that giants eat."

The people broke or cut off hunks of bread, but the slice looked just the same, it was so enormous. They all agreed that the giants' bread did not taste any worse than theirs, but on the other hand, did not taste any better either.

For three whole weeks, the village baked no bread and lived off that slice. But nothing lasts for ever. The bread was eaten and my tale is told.

Rumpelstiltskin

It happened a long time ago, when there was still a great deal of poverty. There lived a mother and two daughters: her own daughter, Elena, and her stepdaughter, Anna. Elena was clumsy and lazy and no one tried to make her otherwise. All the work in and about the house was done by Anna, who was quick and clever with her hands.

Both girls were of a marrying age. Elena had fallen in love with a young man named Adam, a handsome, able lad, but he had eyes only for Anna and Anna for him. If they happened to meet, they forgot everything around them and just gazed into each other's eyes. Elena was eaten up with jealousy.

"Your stepdaughter is ruining my happiness," she complained to her mother. "Adam pays no attention to anyone else. Yesterday evening, when we were spinning, he sat next to her the whole time. He took her hands in his and told her, 'I need these hands of gold in my own house.'"

The stepmother flared up in rage and at once thought of a way of getting rid of Anna. She led her into the little storeroom at the back of the house and said to her, "I've heard you have hands of gold, if that's the case I'll give them work with gold. You will spin all the flax into gold thread! You'll stay in this storeroom until you've finished it."

All of Anna's pleas and tears were in vain, her stepmother shut and bolted the heavy door and left her alone.

It was dark in the storeroom, the tiny window just under the roof hardly let any light in at all. Anna wept bitterly. All the injustices she had stifled in her heart over the years were now flowing out in tears. When at last she stopped crying, she looked up towards the little window, yet not a trace of light was to be seen. This made her despair even more. She caught her head in her hands and cried out,

Night in day and night in night,
Who will help me in my plight?

No sooner had she uttered these words than to her surprise, the wall of the storeroom began to open and outside she could see the dark blue night with the moon and stars. Through this opening in the wall, she saw a beautiful coach, carrying a little man in red trousers with a red hat on his over-large head. The dwarf drove around Anna, then brought his coach to a halt and said, "I'll help you, Anna. I'll teach you to spin gold thread."

"Teach me, dear little dwarf, teach me, please!" Anna cried out in joy.

"I'll teach you, but you must promise that a year and a day from now you will meet me in the same place and try to guess my name. If you guess my name, I don't want you, but if you don't guess it, I'll take you away and you will become my wife. Do you agree to that?"

What could poor Anna do? If she didn't agree, she would never get out of that dark hole. After all, in a year, all kinds of things can happen, and maybe she would even manage to guess the dwarf's name. So she nodded in agreement.

"Well then, sit down at the spinning wheel and spin," said the little man.

Anna set the spindle spinning and he drove around her in his coach, singing at the top of his voice.

Spin the spindle, turn the wheel,
You and I have made a deal.
Thread of gold will set the seal.

At that moment, Anna's thread suddenly glistened, like a ray of sunlight breaking the darkness through a crack in a wall. This ray wound itself round the spindle and the spindle spun and grew. Then, suddenly, the little man came to a halt and said, "Well, Anna, you have become a spinner of gold. I have kept my promise and in a year and a day you must keep yours."

34

Laughing gleefully, he disappeared through the gap in the wall and the wall closed behind him, as if it had never opened.

The next day, when the stepmother opened the storehouse door, she was almost blinded by the glitter of gold. She quickly went into the kitchen, heaped the gold thread into a chest and fastened the lock. She would sell it and her daughter would be the richest bride in the country.

Rumors about the spinner of gold spread like wildfire, not only through the neighbourhood, but throughout the kingdom. Suitors began to arrive at the cottage from far and wide: farmers and foresters, shepherds and soldiers, earls and barons in powdered wigs. Although the stepmother dressed her daughter up like a princess, it was Anna they wanted to marry. Of course the stepmother could not agree to this. She would be a fool indeed to let her stepdaughter spin gold for someone else.

One day a royal procession was seen approaching the cottage. It was the king himself on a white horse. The stepmother realized what he had come for and a daring idea occurred to her. She sent Anna away and sat Elena down at the spinning wheel, pressing the spindle of gold thread into her hand.

"Look as if you are spinning and leave the rest to me," she directed her.

At that very moment, a royal fanfare resounded in front of the house and the king appeared in the doorway.

"Is this the spinner of gold?" he asked.

"Yes, your Royal Highness, this is my daughter, Elena," the stepmother replied.

The king took hold of the spindle, twisted the gold thread around his fingers and thought to himself, "The girl isn't exactly beautiful, but the gold is." However, he said aloud, "Elena? A pretty name, it would suit a queen, too. Madam, give me your daughter's hand in marriage."

The stepmother was beside herself with joy. "It is a great honour for us, Your Majesty."

"Well, prepare your daughter for the journey. In two hours' time, a coach will come to take her to the royal palace."

When the king had left and all that was to be heard was the

retreating hoofs of his company, Elena at last managed to say something. "How could you do that, mother? Am I the spinner of gold?"

"Don't worry, my child," her mother calmed her, beaming with joy. She lost no time and sent for her stepdaughter. Anna was told that Elena was going to marry the king and that they were going to move to the castle. They would leave Anna alone in the cottage, so she could marry Adam. But in return, she must give them all the gold she spun.

Anna was only too willing to agree, because Adam meant more to her than all the gold in the world. Perhaps he would help her guess the name of that terrible dwarf with a big head. The thought of him weighed on her mind more and more as time went by.

The stepmother and Elena wrapped up all the gold thread that was in the house and when the king's coach arrived, they stepped into it, dressed in their most beautiful clothes. They drove in great pomp to the royal palace. There the three gates were opened for them, one after the other, and at the third stood the king to welcome them. He led Elena and her mother into a vast chamber, which was packed high to the ceiling with flax.

"I have prepared for you the best-quality flax to be found in the whole of the land," he explained. "I need an enormous amount of gold, because the royal treasury is empty. You, dear Elena, will save our kingdom from disaster. Within a year and a day, you will spin all this flax into gold, and as soon as you have finished, I'll prepare a royal wedding. Why have you turned so pale, my dear bride?"

"She's overcome with happiness, Your Majesty," the stepmother hastened to explain. "You can rely on us. Everything will be as you wish."

"I hope so, or it will be the worse for you," said the king, a threatening tone creeping into his voice. "In order that no one shall disturb you in your work, I'll lock this chamber and carry the key with me."

"But, Your Majesty, I must go home once more," said the stepmother. "In our haste we forgot something..."

The king allowed her to leave once more and the stepmother, of course, went straight back to the cottage and to Anna. She embraced her and addressed her in a wheedling manner. "Dear girl, now tell me, how did you become a spinner of gold?"

Anna did not want to tell her for anything in the world, because she said it was so terrible and who knew what would come of it. But the old woman would give her no peace until, at last, she had told her everything: how in the night that verse had happened to come to her lips and a dwarf in a red cap had appeared and taught her to spin gold thread. But that was not all, Anna warned her, in a year's time the dwarf would return and she would have to try to guess his name. If she didn't guess it, the dwarf would take her away, who knows where.

This shook the stepmother somewhat, but then she said, "Well, you will have to guess it first. You will guess his name and come and

tell us. People should help each other, my dear." Anna promised to do this and the stepmother returned to the palace. At the stroke of midnight, Elena recited the magic verse,

Night in day and night in night,
Who will help me in my plight?

The dwarf came, taught her to spin gold thread and said that he would return in a year and a day and she must guess his name. If she guessed his name, he wouldn't want her, but if she didn't guess it, he would take her.

Elena spun and spun, the pile of flax getting smaller and smaller. Every day the king came to the chamber to take away the gold thread she had spun. First he filled the royal treasury, then he had gold buttons made for all his clothes, gold swords for the royal guard, gold spurs for the royal cavalry and gold horseshoes for the royal horses. Then he had the roofs of the royal palace guilded, so that on a bright day it looked like the home of the sun itself. The king felt happy in the midst of all this glittering splendour, the only trouble was that he liked his future queen, Elena, less and less. How would it look if he, one of the richest kings in the world, had to sit beside such an ugly queen? If only he could get rid of her. The days passed and there was less and less of the year to go.

Anna married Adam, but a black cloud hung over their happiness. What if she didn't guess the name of the dwarf? She quite gave up weaving gold thread and spent day after day trying to think up all kinds of names.

"Maybe he's called Redcap," said Adam. "Or perhaps Bighead? Or what about Puckelf? What if he's called Flibbertigoblin? Or, you know what? One woman from the other side of the river said that there were once two dwarfs called Fiddle-faddle and Fiddle-de-dee. The trouble is, such a cripple might just as well be called Shortfoot. Or... Pipsqueak."

If Anna had not been so terribly worried, she would have laughed, but as it was, she just shook her head as if to say, no, it could hardly be that, such names didn't seem likely to her at all.

The year passed and just one single day was left. The waiting was more than Adam could bear, so he took his axe and went off into the forest to prepare wood for the fire. He strode on and on, quite

forgetting he was looking for wood and just letting his legs take him wherever they happened to go. It was already getting dark but he still walked on and on, his heart torn with despair. Suddenly, he found himself at the edge of the forest, looking down over a little valley and in the valley, a light was shining. Adam strained his eyes to see and ears to hear.

In the middle of the valley stood a tree with nine branches. On every branch hung a pot and under every pot burned a fire. A dwarf in a red cap was leaping from branch to branch like a grasshopper, stirring first the contents of one pot, then of another, then of a third, singing all the while.

> *The night was dark,*
> *I heard your call,*
> *I came to help,*
> *I taught you all.*
> *Golden thread you spun*
> *That glittered like the sun.*
>
> *The year has passed,*
> *The time has come.*
> *Tonight you guess my name.*
> *Guess it right,*
> *I'll let you go,*
> *Guess it wrong,*
> *You can't say no,*
> *You'll be my wife,*
> *For all your life,*
> *And my name is... RUMPELSTILTSKIN*
> *Ha! ha! ha! ha! ha!*

This was just what Adam needed, he wasted no time and ran back home as fast as his legs would carry him. It was just before midnight when he reached the house and Anna was already waiting in the storeroom. Adam told her what he had seen and heard and hid in a corner behind some sacks, in order to be close at hand, just in case... On the stroke of midnight, the wall in the storeroom opened, the dwarf appeared in his coach and drove around Anna, singing at the top of his voice,

You called for help — I came,
Tonight you guess my name,
Guess it right, I'll let you go,
Guess it wrong, you can't say no!
So guess, Anna, guess!

"I'll try to guess," said Anna. "Your name is Rumpelstiltskin."

The dwarf turned red in rage, tore his hat off his head and flung it onto the floor. There was clap as of thunder and grey smoke filled the room. When it cleared, the wall of the storeroom was closed and there was no trace of the dwarf and no trace of the gold thread either; it had all changed back to ordinary linen yarn. The dwarf had disappeared and Anna's ability to spin gold had gone forever, too. But she did not mind and neither did Adam. They were beside themselves with joy, because they had each other and need not fear the dwarf any longer.

First thing in the morning, Anna hurried to the royal palace to tell Elena the dwarf's name. But, oh dear, the chamber where she spun gold thread was kept locked from morning to night and the king carried the key in his pocket wherever he went.

Anna therefore asked to be led before the king and there, bit by bit, she explained the whole situation.

"So that's how it is," thought the king, "not only have they deceived me, but what's more I'm to lose all my gold?..."

Then he said aloud, "So his name is Rumpelstiltskin. Very well. I'll tell Lady Elena that."

"And couldn't I do it?" asked Anna, "I haven't seen her for such a long time."

"No, Anna, you cannot. Lady Elena and her mother have too much to do getting ready for the royal wedding: the dressmakers, wigmakers and shoemakers are with them right now. Don't worry,

I'll tell them the name. Rumpels-tiltskin — that's it, isn't it?" Then he sent Anna away.

The fateful day approached and Elena and her mother waited impatiently for the message from Anna. The very last day dawned and they just could not wait any longer. They asked the king whether such and such a farmgirl had come looking for them.

"Yes, there was someone of that description. She said her name was Anna and she tried to get to see you, but I didn't allow it. How would it look if an ordinary farmgirl could get to see the queen just at the asking!"

"Ah! But she was to tell us one name!" the stepmother gasped in dismay.

"She did mention a name," said the king. "Such a funny name, it'll make you laugh! Rumpleskin!"

"Rumpleskin?" repeated Elena and her mother in one voice.

"Or was it Rumpigskin? One or the other," said the king and before they could ask anything more, he turned and left, carefully locking the door behind him. But he was burning with curiosity to know what would happen, so when Elena and her mother were having supper he crept back and hid behind a curtain.

At midnight, as soon as the palace clocks began to strike twelve, the wall opened, the little coach came in, carrying the dwarf. He was wearing red trousers and a red hat on his over-large head. He drove once around Elena and said,

> *You called for help — I came,*
> *Tonight you guess my name,*
> *Guess it right, I'll let you go,*
> *Guess it wrong, you can't say no!*
> *So guess, Elena, guess!*

42

"I'll try to guess," said Elena and her voice shook. "Your name is Rumpleskin."

The dwarf laughed, clapping his hands in delight.

"You haven't guessed right, my dear bride, step up into my coach!"

Here the stepmother broke in, "It was just a slip of the tongue. We know your name from Anna, and if it was good enough for her, it must be good enough for us, too."

The dwarf hesitated. "Well, if that's the case, you can guess once more, but that will be the last time!"

"Your name is Rumpigskin," said Elena, almost in a whisper.

The little man burst into peals of laughter and clapped his hands in glee. "You haven't guessed it, my dear bride, step up here!" Then touched her with his finger.

No sooner had he touched her, than Elena began to grow smaller and smaller. First she became a little girl, then a tiny girl, then a tiny little girl and in the end, she was a tiny, tiny little girl, no bigger than the little man in the red cap, and even a little smaller. The dwarf caught her by the hand and pulled her into the carriage.

At first the stepmother was struck dumb, but then she came to her senses and stepped in front of the carriage, "You can't do that, sir! You must turn my daughter back to the person she was, she's going to marry the king, not a little midget like you who doesn't even know his own name. I'm not going to let that happen!" She barred the way, stretching her arms out wide so they could not pass.

The dwarf flew into a rage, his face almost as red as the hat on his head. He pulled a magic wand out of his pocket, waved it towards each corner of the room and proclaimed in an ominous voice,

"Abrakadabra, magrakadabra, rabrakadabra!"

At that the whole room and everything in it turned to stone: the stepmother, the king behind the curtain, the spindle, the yarn and the spinning wheel, the whole room was suddenly as dead and grey as an ancient cave. The only living things in it were just leaving in their carriage, the dwarf in his red cap, embracing his tiny little bride and singing at the top of his voice,

> *You called for help — I came,*
> *You did not guess my name.*

A wedding feast awaits us now.
You have no choice, you'll keep your vow.
And my name is RUMPELSTILTSKIN! Ha! ha! ha! ha!

The next day, the courtiers looked all over the palace for the king, but they couldn't find him anywhere. To their astonishment, they discovered that the chamber in which the king's bride had lived was all of stone, not a living thing in it. There were two rocks which reminded them of human figures, but that one of them should be the king never even occurred to anyone. So they waited a whole week and three days for the king who did not return. Since the country needed a ruler, they crowned the king's younger brother, who had long dreamed of taking his brother's place.

The new king began to live so much like a king that, in a very short time, he had emptied the king's treasury, no matter how full it had been. The royal horses soon wore out their golden horseshoes. The royal guards gambled away their golden swords and the royal cavalry wasted their golden spurs on drink. The gilt on the palace roofs was washed away by the rain.

Every time the king wanted to send for a jug of wine, he had to tear a gold button off his robes. But there were soon none left.

The only income the royal treasury had was from travelers, who came from far and wide to admire the stone chamber and try, in vain, to explain the mystery of its origin.

The Little Key on the Blue Ribbon

Far away, at the very edge of the world, where the world ends and where it begins, there was a land called Cantahiri, whose king was named Mohai. For many years, King Mohai had no son or heir, and when one was born at last, he was beside himself with joy. He named him Christian after his own father and it now seemed that he could not be happier. But that was not the case.

The very day he was born, someone hung a little key on a blue ribbon around the baby's neck.

"Who dared to do such a thing!" King Mohai cried in anger. "The only things that are locked up are locked up because I want them to be, so what is the need of a key!" He ordered the nurse to throw the key away. The nurse threw the little key into the dustbin and even emptied the ashes over it. But, at that very moment, the key was found hanging round the little prince's neck, as if it had been there all the time. Seeing that, the king gave an order for it to be buried in the garden, and he himself would see to it that they dug the hole deep enough. They buried the key seven and a half fathoms deep and trod down the earth on top of it, but when they returned to the palace, it was once more hanging around the royal neck.

"Throw it into the fire!" shouted King Mohai.

So they tried to burn the key. Then they broke it and crushed it and tried to get rid of it in all kinds of other ways but to no avail. Every time the little key returned to little Prince Christian and hung itself around his neck.

In the end, King Mohai had to give up. "Let it!" he shrugged. That meant, let it hang there. Anyway, the little key was always hidden under the prince's royal robes, so it almost looked as if it didn't exist. But it did. King Mohai could not forget it for a minute.

Prince Christian grew. They had long stopped calling him little Prince Christian, everyone called him Crown Prince Christian. He was so tall and so grave. As if he was always thinking about something. About what? King Mohai would have given anything to know what his son, Christian, was thinking about and what he did when he was alone. But the prince kept his heart a secret from him.

Now King Mohai had a talking bird. Every afternoon, when dinner was over, the king used to stay at the table and talk to his bird.

"And what did my son do today?" he would ask every day.

"Today the Prince chose to have a lesson of mathematics, then he listened to a lecture on the history of our famous empire, Cantahiri, then he had a fencing lesson..."

"Go on, go on..." the king would say impatiently.

"And then, sire, Crown Prince Christian tried several more doors in the palace to see whether the little key on the blue ribbon would fit."

"Not again," King Mohai sighed.

"Again, sire. He has now tried them all, but the key doesn't fit any of them. Then Crown Prince went into the garden and stood for

a long, long time gazing at the tea rose that grows in the farthermost corner of the garden.

"I don't like him wandering around like that, I don't like it at all!" exclaimed the king. "And what did they talk about?"

"I'm afraid I don't know. It was a meeting without words. I was sitting very close to the bush, so I know that for sure. The rose only let out its sweet scent and the prince shook his head as if he didn't understand..."

"I don't like it! Why are there roses there anyway?" the king asked angrily. "Don't let the prince out of your sight, my dear friend, and tell me whatever you find out at once."

"I am always at your service, Your Majesty," the bird bowed its head.

The next day, when Crown Prince Christian went to see the tea rose, he found the whole of the far end of the garden had been cut down and laid waste. There was no trace of the rose bushes anywhere. The only thing he found, a little way away from the spot where it had been growing, was the tea rose, crushed and trodden into the ground. He lifted it and placed it gently in his palm like an injured bird and the rose let out a fragrance more beautiful than ever. It was trying to tell him something before it wilted away forever. So fervently and urgently did it speak that at last the prince understood. All of a sudden her message was quite clear!

"In the secret corner of the garden, behind the screen of alder trees," said the rose, "is a wall, behind which, on every thirteenth day, quiet sobs can be heard. Find that wall and touch it with the little key on the blue ribbon." There was more to what she said, but it was spoken in such a faint whisper that it was impossible to hear.

The prince kissed the dying rose, placed it gently in a soft dip in the ground and hurried off to the secret corner of the garden. He passed through the dark screen of alder trees and found himself in front of a towering, thick, grey wall. The prince drew near, pulled out the key on the blue ribbon, which all his life he had worn next to his heart and touched the wall with it.

Hardly had he done so when a dull, cracking sound was heard, like the cracking of ice on the river at the end of winter. A crevice appeared in the wall, which grew wider and wider, first like a window and then like a wide gate. Out of that gate stepped a maiden! Her hair and clothes were covered with green mould, her face was marked with suffering, but her eyes shone with happiness like the hot sun.

"I am Princess Christiana and I thank you for setting me free," she said fervently. She stretched out her arms towards the prince and he took her in his arms and kissed her.

At that moment, as if at a secret signal, the wind began to blow through the crack in the wall. It howled in the tops of the alder trees, whistled around the chimneys and swept through the windows of the royal palace. King Mohai was just having his lunch and his bird was hopping up and down in the anteroom waiting to break some very disturbing news to the king... when the windows and doors of the dining hall were blown in, the royal crown was whisked off the royal head and rolled over and over in the direction of the doors. King Mohai gasped in horror, his hands flying to his head, and up he jumped to chase his crown! The crown clattered down the stairs, leaping ten steps at a time, flew through the palace gates and off down the street with the king behind it. He looked neither to left nor right, his eyes just fixed on the crown that rolled in front of him, on he ran as people laughed, for without his crown they didn't recognize their king, all they saw was a crazy old man, a napkin under his chin, dashing down the road with a peculiar bird flapping at his heels...

Crown Prince Christian led Princess Christiana back to the royal palace. People came out to meet him calling, "Welcome, Crown Prince Christian. You have come just in time. Your father, King Mohai, has lost his royal crown, so take your place on the throne."

"So it came true after all!" exclaimed Princess Christiana.

"What came true?"

"King Mohai was once told by a fortune teller that the moment someone kissed me, he would lose his crown. That is why he had me walled up."

48

"Forget all your suffering, dear," said Prince Christian. He and Christiana stepped up to the throne of the empire of Cantahiri and gave their first two royal commands: to knock down and clear away the grey wall in the hidden corner of the garden and to abolish all secret nooks!

Ever since that time, in the empire of Cantahiri, the sun shines into every corner and crevice, the wind blows into every nook and justice reaches all. Long live King Christian!

Pretty Susan and the Water Sprite

Give me your hand, shut your eyes, my little friend, and I'll take you along rugged paths, through shady groves, across green fields, and here we are. Can you hear the music? The river is remembering the melody the water sprite once played on his gold violin.

The water sprite used to sit in the branches of a willow tree and he would sing. Over there, on the other side of the river stood a little cottage, dilapidated and poverty-stricken, because the people who lived there were as poor as church mice: a woodcutter with his wife and a swarm of children. They managed, more or less, to feed them, but clothes and shoes were beyond their means. Greater poverty you cannot find even in a fairytale.

It was their daughter, Susan, who found it hardest to bear this poverty. She was as pretty as a picture; if she had dressed up in fine clothes and appeared at the manorhouse ball, young men would have drawn their swords to win her favour. But this Susan had to go round in a patched-up skirt and tattered blouse. For the most part, she went barefoot, because she had to share the only boots in the house with her two other sisters, and that only on Sundays. Nevertheless, Susan's beauty was not lost even in her shabby clothes, it radiated from her face, her hair, her figure and her walk.

The water sprite's eyes were drawn to pretty Susan. Every time she crossed the bridge over the river, he looked down on her through the branches of an old willow and his eyes lit up like fire. He wasn't old yet, only three hundred years, and for water sprites that is the best age. He would sit in that willow, play his gold violin and sing this song.

A crystal palace is all my own,
With silken walls and silver floors,
Fish and waves are at my call,

50

And make my bed of soft, white foam.
I've gold and pearls and precious stones,
Whate'er I want, I have it all.
There is but one for whom I yearn,
For a pretty wife my heart does burn.

Once, when Susan was crossing the footbridge, he called to her from his willow tree, "Hey, there Susan!" When she stopped for a moment, he added, "Susan, marry me and be my wife!"

Susan just called over her shoulder, "How can I marry when I haven't got what is needed!"

"And what is needed?"

"Eiderdowns, sheets, poplin, ribbons, everything a young bride should have, of course."

"If that is all, you shall have it by the morning," said the water sprite happily.

The next morning, when the family was up and about, there were cries of surprise and wonder when they saw what was in the yard. The trees around were adorned with lengths of fine white linen, calico, all colours of the rainbow, red poplin, chiffon, batiste, cambric, percale and velvet. Ribbons, laces and rows of pearls hung from the branches and the well was draped with a piece of fine green cloth, such as was used in those days for wedding skirts.

At first, the sight struck Susan with fear, but she soon took courage. Together with her sisters, she gathered up this wealth and packed it away in wooden chests. Then they all set to work to sew skirts, blouses and bodices. From that time on, they were so handsomely dressed that not even the village mayor's daughter could compare to them. But Susan took great care not to go near the river and kept well away from the footbridge.

Once, however, she had to go that way, and then she heard a voice coming from the willow, "Hey there, Susan, when are you going to marry me?"

"Oh, I can't marry yet," Susan managed to force a smile. "I have nothing to offer the guests at the wedding feast."

"If that is all!" the water sprite called out joyfully, "you'll have it tomorrow."

In the early hours of the morning, the village was woken by the sound of rushing water, screams and cries and hullabaloo. The stream had broken its banks and the muddy waters swirled and dashed, gushing and rushing, carrying off logs, fences, bridges, henhouses with their poultry, and pigpens with their pigs. Wonder of wonders, they were all swept into Susan's yard. The waters brought her a pile of wood higher than the roof, pigs, poultry and even a bullock and a heifer. It would have been enough not for one wedding but for five at least.

This time Susan really took fright. What if the water sprite should force her to marry him?

She hurried off to see a wise woman who lived seven villages away.

"Good woman, look what trouble I am in, could you advise me what to do?"

"Dear girl, you should have come for advice before you began to make fun of the water sprite," the wise woman rebuked her. "But perhaps there is something I can do to help you. Take this little white herb, sew it into your clothes and wear it always close to your heart. The white herb will keep the water sprite and all other evils away."

Susan rewarded the wise woman well and from then on she went nowhere without the white herb. She lived in peace, not catching even a glimpse of the water sprite, because he had not the power to come close to her. In time, she married a handsome young man and they were happy together. Susan only begged her husband to keep away from any kind of water when he was out of the house, and he readily promised her that.

One day, however, he was coming back from the fields and he was so terribly thirsty, he just couldn't wait until he got home. So he turned off the path across the meadow and knelt down beside a spring to take a sip of water. But his lips had hardly touched the surface when something caught him by the tongue. It was the water sprite.

"Promise to give me what you have at home, but don't know about," he said in a deep voice, "otherwise I shall pull you down into my watery kingdom."

"If I don't know I have it, I suppose I won't miss it very much," thought Susan's husband and he nodded in agreement. At that, the water sprite let him go and he set off for home.

Give me your hand, my little friend, we are going there with him. How your heart is beating! That is because you feel what your mind has not yet grasped, that what we have at home that we don't know about is often the most important thing of all.

When the husband came home, his wife said to him, "I have good news for you, dear! Before next spring there will be three of us."

But Susan's husband did not welcome the news at all. His heart missed a beat and his eyes filled with tears, for he realized then that he had just promised the water sprite his own child, which had not yet been born. When he told Susan what had happened, she was overcome with grief, and from then on, her right eye never stopped shedding tears.

The baby was happily born and it was a beautiful little boy. His mother immediately sewed the white herb into his shirt, to keep the water sprite and all other evils away from him. The boy grew, he was healthy, handsome and good. He was only sorry that his parents had strictly forbidden him to go down to the river.

Thus his twelfth birthday came and went. One day the other boys went down to the river to bathe. At first, Susan's son just stood on the bank and watched the others splashing about in the water. All of a sudden, he was seized by an irresistible longing to join them. It made him forget his parents' prohibition, he took off his clothes and put them under a bush together with the white herb that protected him. He had hardly entered the water when something pulled him down beneath the surface and he was never seen again, dead or alive.

This terrible misfortune made his mother's other eye shed tears and it never stopped from that time on. It did not even stop when the old forester from the valley came to tell her that once in the light of the moon he had caught sight of a water sprite, a very young sprite that looked so much like her son.

From that time, Susan would go down to the river and sit under the willow from early in the evening to late at night, but she was never lucky enough to see either her son or the old water sprite.

The sound of his gold violin was no more to be heard, nor his song of love. But the river had learned it long ago and sometimes on a moonlit night, like that of tonight, it quietly sings. Listen!

> *A crystal palace is all my own,*
> *With silken walls and silver floors,*
> *Fish and waves are at my call,*
> *And make my bed of soft, white foam.*
> *I've gold and pearls and precious stones,*
> *Whate'er I want, I have it all.*
> *There is but one for whom I yearn,*
> *For a pretty wife my heart does burn.*

The Children and the Dragon

Under a rock in a deep, deep valley, there once lived a dragon. At one time, he had been an enormous snake, but when he was two hundred years old, wings began to grow on his back. They grew bigger and bigger, bigger and bigger, so that by the time another hundred years had passed, they had grown into dragon's wings and the snake was no longer just a snake, it was a real live dragon. His back was hard and cracked like the bark of an old, old tree and his tail was so long and so terribly strong!

This dragon was the oldest of all the snakes, so they made him their king. But even though he was a king, he, too, had a master he had to obey. His lord and master was the Wizard.

The Wizard had a Black Book with all kinds of wonderful spells. He only had to read out one of these magic verses and the dragon had to come crawling out from under his rock whether he wanted to or not. The Wizard would then throw a bridle over his head, get up on his back and they would soar off high into the sky. They flew along like a fiery cloud, the dragon lashing his powerful tail and leaving a whirlwind of destruction behind him.

The dragon hated people and would have been glad to get rid of them all. But the Wizard could not let this happen, because people used to give him eggs from coal-black hens and that was his favorite food. They gave him milk from jet-black cows and that was his favorite drink. That is why he tried to protect people from the dragon's anger.

They flew on and on, the countryside below stretching far and wide in all directions, and every few moments the dragon would bellow, "Where are we now? What is down there?"

"We are flying over a forest," the Wizard would say, as they passed a village and fields.

The dragon liked the forest; he had grown up in the forest and did not want to harm it. So he restrained his anger and flew on calmly.

The people in the villages and fields pressed their hands to their mouths in fear. Only the children whispered in wonder:

> *Look there, look there,*
> *It's a dragon in the air.*
> *The Wizard's astride him,*
> *How long will he ride him?*
> *The clouds are on fire,*
> *When will he tire?*

Very soon the dragon would bellow again, "Where are we now? What is below us?"

A forest stretched far and deep below them, but the Wizard said, "We are flying over villages and fields."

Hearing this, the dragon began to lash his tail so furiously that at every sweep, he sent trees crashing to the ground. Everything around clamored, groaned and wailed as if the world was coming to an end.

The dragon flew on and on until his rage was spent and then, at the Wizard's command, he tamely returned to his hollow under a rock in the deep valley.

But what should happen one day!

Who knows how it came about, but one day the Wizard forgot to lock the chest where he always kept his Black Book. He just closed the lid and went to bed.

Well, his two children, a boy and girl, had been waiting for just that moment for a long time. Before you could say Jack Robinson, they had taken the book, leafed through it and hit on the page with the

56

magic verse. The boy already knew how to read, so he lost no time and read it aloud:

> *Call out, call out —*
> *"Snake king! Snake king!*
> *Crawl out, crawl out,*
> *Spread your wing, spread your wing!"*

No sooner had he said it, the dragon crawled out from under his rock, spread his wings and soared up into the sky.

You can imagine what happened next!

The trees in the gardens and fields were torn up by their roots like weak little saplings, roofs and chimneys came toppling to the ground, everything spun and whirled as if it were boiling in a hellish cauldron.

People saw that the dragon had no rider and were frightened to death. The braver ones went from house to house collecting eggs from coal-black hens and milk from jet-black cows, and hurrying as fast as their legs would carry them to the Wizard's house.

"Where is your father?" they asked the children.

"He's asleep," said the children, hurriedly putting back the Black Book, sensing there was going to be trouble.

The people tried to wake the Wizard up, but he was sound asleep. They had to pull his nose and even tickle the soles of his feet before he would open his eyes.

"What do you want?" he grunted irritably, annoyed at being interrupted in his sleep. But when he saw the eggs from coal-black hens and milk from jet-black cows, his anger quite disappeared.

"Call back the dragon, please, please! Call him back, or it will be the end of all of us!" the people begged.

The Wizard opened his chest, took out the Black Book and read out these magic words:

> *Snake king, snake king!*
> *Fold your wing, fold your wing!*
> *You've caused enough sorrow,*
> *Crawl back to your hollow!*

In a short while, the dragon calmed down and it seemed that he would obey but then he flew once more into a rage. He was so much enjoying it without his lord and master that he wanted to see what would happen if he did not do as he was told.

But the Wizard called to him a second time, and then a third in a loud, commanding voice:

> *Snake king, snake king!*
> *Fold your wing, fold your wing!*
> *Crawl back to your hollow,*
> *You can come out tomorrow!*

These words had such a powerful effect that the dragon just had to obey. He even came back like a shamefaced dog with his tail between his legs. Having quietly landed on the ground, he tamely crawled back under his rock in the deep, deep valley.

Simon and Odetta

There was once a girl as lovely as a flower. Fleet of foot, quick of mind, with coal-black eyes and cheeks like roses. Her name was very beautiful, too. She was called Odetta.

Young men from far and wide tried to win her favour, but she had eyes only for her beloved Simon. Simon was as tall, straight and strong as a fir tree and what is more, he had a good heart. His only fault was that he had not a penny to his name, neither a hen nor a pen. What could he do with a hen if he had no yard to keep it in? And what was the use of a pen without pigs? Simon had nothing in the world he could call his own, he just served one master or another, as chance would have it.

Odetta, however, did not mind this in the least. Her heart beat with joy when Simon appeared at her window, pressed her hand in his and spoke words of affection in her ear. But her father and mother saw the matter in a very different light. They spent all of their time thinking of ways to part the two forever.

In the end, they thought of something.

One day, when Odetta was not at home, her father edged her window frame with the blades of sharp knives and razors. When Simon came in the evening and stretched out his hand to knock on the window, he almost cut his hand to ribbons.

Simon strode off in anger, thinking that Odetta had prepared this trap for him. He disappeared from sight, he disappeared from the village, no one had any idea where he could have gone.

Odetta, of course, guessed what had happened when in the morning she found blood on her window sill and knives and razors stuck in the frame. She said nothing to her mother and father, but secretly made a bundle of her things and one morning, while it was still dark outside, she set out into the world to look for her own dear Simon.

She trudged along roads and paths, in the heat, the rain and the wind, asking every single person she met whether they had seen a strong, handsome, well-built young man. But no one had.

After walking and walking a long, long time, Odetta came to a castle. It looked deserted, uninhabited, but the gates opened for her as she approached and so she went inside. The castle was full of riches, but not one human being to be seen, only a large green bird flying up and down, calling: "Cum-me, cum-me", as if it wanted Odetta to follow it.

She followed it from chamber to chamber, hall to hall, each more beautiful than the last, golden tables everywhere, gold dishes on the tables and shining armour on the walls. Odetta came to the last room and found it full of costly robes, but all for men. She dressed herself up in these clothes, put on a belt with three round buckles and fastened a golden sword at her side. She looked at herself in a mirror and saw that she looked quite like a prince, and a handsome prince at that, in a shining array. The green bird flew round her all the time, uttering its strange call: "Cum-me, cum-me" as if he still wanted her to follow him. Odetta let the bird lead her to the stables, where four beautiful stallions were shaking their manes and pawing the ground. Odetta harnessed the stallions onto the coach and off they galloped! They flew as if on wings until they came to a halt in the courtyard of an inn in a royal town. Odetta handed over the reins to a servant and went inside the inn, ordered lunch and asked, "Well, good sir, tell me what is new."

"Well, the latest news," said the innkeeper, "is that our princess is marrying a young man who freed her from a dragon. The wedding should take place this very day, but the best man has fallen ill. So, who knows how they will manage at the wedding."

Then the innkeeper took a closer look at his guest and suddenly said, "Young man, would you be willing to act as best man?"

"Why not?!" Odetta replied.

The innkeeper sent a message to the palace and a ministerial adviser came hurrying back from there, explaining that it was like this and like that, and in short that the king and the princess begged the young man to act as best man.

Odetta arrived at the royal wedding, caught sight of the bridegroom and almost fainted on the spot! It was Simon, who she had been looking for so long and been unable to find. She was so overcome with grief that one of the gold buckles on her belt burst in two.

"What was that burst?" asked the first bridesmaid.

Odetta answered, "Burst, buckle, burst! Odetta's heart must burst when her beloved one is marrying another!"

But the bridesmaid did not catch what the best man said, she just adjusted the gold edging on her costly robe.

Then Odetta approached the young bride, and when she gazed into her radiant face, the second buckle burst on her gold belt.

"What was that bursting sound?" asked the princess.

And Odetta answered, "Burst, buckle, burst! Odetta's heart must burst when her beloved one is marrying another!"

The princess did not hear what she said either. At that particular moment she was not interested in anything anyone said.

The best man led the young bride to the bridegroom in front of the altar, and as she came near to him, the third buckle on her belt burst.

"What's that burst?" asked the bridegroom.

Odetta replied, "Burst, buckle, burst. Odetta's heart must burst when her beloved one is marrying another!"

Simon turned to look the best man in the face and all of a sudden, he recognized his own dear Odetta and saw that she was near fainting. He caught her by the hands, turned to the king and the princess and said, "That is how it is and it can never be otherwise: this is not my bride standing here with a gold wreath in her hair. This is my bride, whose heart is bursting with grief. My dearest Odetta."

Hand in hand, Simon and Odetta stepped up before the altar. Later, in the courtyard of the inn, they got into their coach harnessed to the four stallions who were shaking their manes and pawing the ground.

Their magic horse flew back like a whirlwind to that deserted castle, where the gate opened for them as they approached. The big green bird was waiting for them on the threshold flapping its wings and calling in its powerful voice, "Cum-me, cum-me." Odetta, full of gratitude, flung her arms around it, stroking it and kissing it on the beak. At that instant, the green bird changed into an old man dressed in the rich robes of a prince.

"Welcome young man, young woman, to my castle, which from now on will be yours," said the old prince. "For a whole two centuries I have waited for this moment and at last it has come. I was once young and handsome like you, but I behaved badly to a girl that loved me. I betrayed her and she laid a curse on me, that I should fly around my castle like a green bird until the time I helped another couple to attain happiness. I waited long, oh, how long, for in this world, true love is far rarer than gold, far rarer than precious stones. It is the greatest treasure of all, so guard it well."

With these words, he quietly passed away, as when a candle burns itself out.

Simon and Odetta prepared a fine funeral for the old man and then stayed on to live in the castle. It was not long before the castle was full of life. Flowers blossomed all around, coaches rattled through the gates and in a year or two the halls and gardens resounded with the laughter of young children.

Simon and Odetta lived happily ever after. They had so much love it would have been enough for three lives. They are still living today. Do you want to know where? In that country, where they do not say of happy couples that "they live together like a pair of turtle doves," but that "they live together like Simon and Odetta." Well, there.

Johnny Pea

No sooner had Johnny Pea arrived in this world than he decided he liked it. But his mother wrung her hands, "Oh, my goodness, what a tiny little boy he is, no bigger than a pea! What will become of him?" She burst into tears, because she hadn't even enough money for the christening, the pantry was empty and the family in debt.

The little boy, truly the size of a pea, jumped to his feet so that his mother could see him better and said, "Don't you worry, Mummy, I'll see to everything!"

He ran out of the cottage and went straight into the forest. There he caught a wild boar and carried it home on his shoulders.

"Now you can prepare a feast, we'll have a proper christening. And give me the name, Johnny Pea."

Just then his father returned from the fields and asked, "Well, what have we, a boy or a girl?"

"Neither a boy, nor a girl," shouted Johnny Pea, making the walls shake, "a real man has been born."

Then he sat down at the table with his father. They ate and drank, his father one dishful, Johnny two, his father one jugful, Johnny two.

"I can see you really are a man," said his father, "and as that's the case, tomorrow we shall go ploughing together."

Johnny knew that ploughing was work for real men.

They arrived at the field. Johnny Pea jumped up into the ox's ear and shouted "giddy-up", urging it to pull the plough. To see them ploughing, you would think they were just playing. When Johnny's father saw that they could manage well without him, he stretched out under a tree, his hat pulled over his eyes, and snored as if he were sawing through a tree.

The lord of the manor happened to pass by on his horse.

"Hey, peasant, what do you think you're doing, snoring here?!" he poked him with his riding cane. "Look, your oxen are trudging up and down the field by themselves!"

Johnny's father jumped up and bowed to the lord.

"They are not trudging by themselves, sir, my son Johnny is driving them."

The lord stared, his eyes opening wide, because he could see no son anywhere. But Johnny kept calling out, "Giddy-up, giddy-up!"

"Well, he can be heard," said the lord, "but I can't see him anywhere. Where is he, for God's sake?"

"He is sitting in the ox's ear, your grace."

The lord went nearer, peered into the ox's ear and his eyes lit up like a hawk's.

"Who'd have believed it? Such a tiny little boy! Sell him to me, I'll give you twenty ducats for him!"

"I can't sell him, your grace, although I need the money badly!"

"A hundred ducats then! And I warn you, take them while they're offered, or you could find you don't get anything at all!"

Hearing this, Johnny winked at his father and whispered, "Sell me, Dad, I'll run away from him!"

With a heavy heart, his father agreed. The lord pulled a purse out of his coat, counted out one hundred ducats, thrust Johnny Pea into the bag with the rest of his money and off he galloped! He just couldn't wait to see his wife's face when he brought her this live toy.

It was dark and cramped inside the bag and no air came in. Johnny Pea pulled out his knife and rip! He cut a hole in the bag and in the lord's pocket, too. Now he could breathe more easily. At once he began to throw out ducat after ducat after ducat. When the purse was empty, he jumped out, too. Back he ran along the road, gathering up the ducats as he went. By the time he reached home, he had a fine pile of them.

"Well, Dad, here's your son and more ducats, too," he said to his father. But his father shook his head, "No good will come of this, son!"

His mother happened to be making dumplings. Johnny's tummy

was already rumbling from hunger, so he jumped up on the stove, then took a flying leap onto the saucepan handle, from where he caught the dumplings floating on the surface of the boiling water. He just could not satisfy his hunger.

At that moment, heavy footsteps were heard in front of the cottage, as if a regiment was approaching. The door flew open and in strode the lord with soldiers at his heels. That artful little devil of a boy had escaped, and what's more, had stolen all his money, too! As sure as eggs are eggs, he must have returned home, so they must give him up at once!

Johnny whispered to his mother, "Put the lid on the saucepan!"

His mother did so.

The lord looked for Johnny Pea, the soldiers looked for Johnny Pea, together they turned the cottage inside out, the only place it did not occur to them to look was in the saucepan. It certainly was hot in there!

They did not find him, but they found his father's ducats and confiscated them all. They even led away the oxen from the stable as a fine, they said. The lord threatened that he would catch that rascal yet!

When they had left at last, Johnny's mother quickly lifted the lid of the saucepan. Johnny Pea jumped out and went reeling about the room, overcome with the heat.

But soon it passed, he even felt stronger than before, as if the boiling water had hardened him like steel.

"Dear mother and father," he said, "I must leave you. If the lord of the manor caught me, I would only bring you bad luck. I'll go out into the world and I won't return until I can repay you all you have lost."

His parents wrung their hands, because they had become very fond of their little son. But they had to admit that he was right and so they saw him off into the world.

He was going through this wide, wide world, and when he had already gone a long way, he caught up with some wagoners. They had seven wagons heaped up with iron.

"Good day to you, good fellows!" he greeted them.

They looked down at him and burst into roars of laughter. "A pea rolling along the road and pretending to be a man!" cried one. "Squash him underfoot!"

"So that's it, is it?" thought Johnny and he was so angry that he suddenly found he had the strength of thirty men. He spat on his palms, pushed his shoulder against the hillside and sent it crashing and tumbling down right across the middle of the road.

The wagoners began to lament, what should they do now, stay there or turn back?

"That's all because you made fun of that little man and didn't return his greeting," said one of them. "Run after him and beg him to come back and help us."

Immediately two of them ran after Johnny Pea and begged him, implored him, to help them. So he went back and said, "I'll clear the road for you if you give me in return as much iron as I can carry away on my shoulders."

They agreed.

Johnny Pea leaned against the mound of earth, not even bothering to spit on his hands this time and he pushed it to one side as easily as if it had been a lump of butter. Now for that iron!

They began piling it up on his shoulders. They emptied the first wagon and were soon taking the last pieces from the second and third.

"Well, isn't that enough for you?"

"Pile it on, pile it on. I can jump over a tree with what you have given me so far." To prove it, he leapt over a two-year fir tree. The wagoners had to empty all the seven wagons and Johnny strode off with this iron, whistling as he went.

He came to a forge and dumped the iron in the yard. As it came crashing down, the ground shook as if there was an earthquake. The blacksmith came running out of his forge. "What is happening? Is the world coming to an end?"

"The world's not coming to an end," said Johnny Pea, "I've just brought you some iron to make into a cudgel for me."

The blacksmith roared with laughter.

"You brought that iron? A little mite like you, who couldn't pick up a feather! Where do little crumbs like you come from?"

This infuriated Johnny.

"You'll regret what you say, if you don't look out!" he shouted, and seizing the iron in his arms, he threw it over the roof of the forge to land on the other side. When it thudded to the ground, the forge jumped in the air a good two feet.

At this the blacksmith began to beg him to forgive him for the insult and not to be angry with him.

"I'll forgive you if you forge me a cudgel out of this iron. Can you do that?"

It took four and twenty journeymen to make the cudgel. While they worked, Johnny Pea and the blacksmith sat at the table, eating and drinking: for every dish the blacksmith ate, Johnny ate three, for every mug of beer the blacksmith drank, Johnny drank five. In the end, the blacksmith was dead drunk, while Johnny was completely sober.

Four and twenty days passed and the four and twenty journeymen finished the cudgel. It weighed ninety-nine tons and just fitted into Johnny's fist.

He paid a fair sum for the work and other expenses and went on his way. He was going along, when he suddenly noticed he had worn

out his boots, and his toes were sticking out of them! He put his cudgel down beside him and sat down under a mushroom, so that the sun would not shine in his eyes. He pulled some thread out of his pocket and began to sew up the holes.

While he was doing this, a man happened to pass. He stopped just beside the mushroom and was about to sit down.

"Look out!" called Johnny. "Don't sit down here — someone'll get hurt!"

The man looked all around him, but he couldn't see under the mushroom. He thought he must have been hearing things, so he went to sit down after all. Johnny stuck out his needle and pricked him through his pants. The man leapt up, howling in pain and fright and took to his heels.

"I told you someone was here!" Johnny called after him, but the man was so terrified that he was afraid to look around.

Johnny then finished sewing up his boots in peace and set off deeper into the forest. Suddenly, he came to a clearing, where a large fire was burning. There were eleven robbers sitting around the fire and roasting a whole ox over the flames. He scrambled up a fir tree and looked down at them. They had just finished roasting the ox and the mouthwatering smell wafted for miles around. They rolled out a barrel of wine from under a bush and began to eat and drink their fill. Johnny chose this moment to pick a cone off a branch and fling it at one of the robbers, just as he was putting his mug to his lips. "You think you're going to swill down wine, while I'm dying of thirst?" He knocked the mug out of his hand. Then he did the same to a second, a third, and so on, right up to the eleventh.

The robbers started up in anger, gazing around to see who was making fools of them. When they had looked in vain for long enough, Johnny slid down to the ground and called to them, "If it interests you, it's me you're looking for."

"And what on earth are you?" they asked.

"A robber like you."

At this, they all roared with laughter, "Just look at him! A robber of the pea family! Nine of them born in one peapod!"

They held their sides, shrieking and hooting. Who knows when they would have stopped, if Johnny had not taken his cudgel and beat

70

them with it. This sobered them up immediately and they accepted him as one of them, offering him roast meat and wine.

The next morning, the robbers were to choose their leader, but they did not know how to go about. it. One suggested one thing, another something else. Finally Johnny Pea said, "Why so much discussion? All of you throw your cudgels in the air and whoever's takes the longest to fall, let him be the leader."

To this they all agreed.

One after the other, they threw up their cudgels and as, so they said, Johnny was now one of them, he should throw his too. Johnny didn't wait to be asked twice, he whirled his cudgel over his head once, twice and flung it up into the air. They waited and waited for the cudgel to fall. In the end, they gave up and lay down to sleep. When they got up in the morning, the cudgel still had not fallen back to earth. It was about noon when it came crashing down from the sky like thunder, boring such a deep hole in the ground that it quite disappeared from sight.

So there was nothing the robbers could do but to accept Johnny as their leader, although they were not very pleased about it at all. He was even more unhappy because he kept thinking about his cudgel. In the end, he said, "The truth of the matter is, we won't get anywhere so long as my cudgel is buried in the ground." So he ordered them to dig. Three days they dug, until they reached somewhere near the gates of hell, and even then, only the very tip of the cudgel could be seen. But that was enough for Johnny. He took a firm grip of the end and pulled it out at once. Then he felt happy again.

Now there was in that country

a splendid royal castle, decorated with silver and precious stones and covered with tiles of gold. But the inside of the castle, there are no words to describe its magnificence. The robbers had tried more than once to get into the castle, but they could get no nearer than a mile away when the cock on the golden roof began to crow, waking up everyone in the castle, so that by the time the robbers got there, the castle guard was waiting for them. All they ever got away with was bruises and bloody wounds.

"We should have another go at the castle, now we have such a strong leader," said one of the robbers.

"Let's try," said Johnny, thinking to himself, "I could certainly do with some gold, at least I could buy my father a pair of oxen."

But he didn't like the thought of having to walk all the way to the castle.

"The castle is a long way off," he said, "and as leader, it wouldn't be fitting for me to have to walk there and carry my cudgel as well."

He gave the order for ten of the robbers to carry his cudgel and he jumped into the pocket of the eleventh. The pocket was deep and dark and it reeked of garlic. Every few minutes Johnny hopped out, gathered up all kinds of stones and piled them up in the pocket until it was full and he could sit on top.

"What's so heavy there?" the robber wondered and went to put his hand to his pocket. But Johnny pushed his hand away each time, "Don't touch your leader!"

When the robber's knees began to give way under the burden, Johnny Pea leapt up on to his cap and laughed as if he had hired him. But the robber was in no laughing mood, and the others, who were carrying his cudgel, looked angrily at him, too. Their shoulders were bruised and aching from the load.

When they were exactly one mile and one stride away from the castle, they came to a halt. Johnny twirled the cudgel around his head and swoosh! He knocked the cock off the roof before it had time to squeal. Thus they could steal quietly up to the castle. Johnny Pea slipped inside through the keyhole and tiptoed over to the window to let in his companions. Just as he was about to open it, he heard them whispering outside, "Now he hasn't got his cudgel with him, he's quite weak, we can easily overpower him and get rid of the little brat."

"You're fine friends, you are," thought Johnny Pea, but he pretended he hadn't heard anything. The first robber was just pulling himself in through the window when he received a sharp blow over

the head, which left him lying stunned on the floor. The same happened to the next and the next and the next, until they all lay in a pile at Johnny Pea's feet. For safety's sake, he tied them up, hand and foot, and then made his way up into the royal chambers.

He had himself announced to the king.

"Your Majesty, there are robbers in your storeroom."

The king took fright and ordered the alarm to be sounded.

"But the robbers are tied up," said Johnny.

The king was delighted and hurried off to see the robbers. They were still lying stiff and stunned.

"And who caught them?" he asked. "These rascals have been keeping me awake at night for years."

"I caught them myself, Your Royal Highness," said Johnny Pea. And he told him all about it.

The king looked him up and down.

"Maybe it was as you say, but you must prove it."

"I can do that at once," said Johnny. "Just order your servants to look for my cudgel and bring it here."

The king sent his servants to look for Johnny's cudgel. When they came back about an hour later, they said, "The cudgel is about half a mile away from the castle, stuck in the ground. But it is terribly heavy. We can't pull it out without horses."

"Well, harness two horses to it," said the king, giving Johnny a look of respect and admiration.

Some time later the servants came back again. "We harnessed your two strongest horses to it, Your Highness, but the cudgel didn't budge an inch."

"Then use four horses," ordered the king, staring thoughtfully at Johnny Pea as if he suspected a trick of some kind.

Again the servants returned, "Your Majesty, we harnessed the four best horses in the royal stables, but they could hardly move the cudgel three inches."

The king was getting impatient, "Well, take six horses and bring the cudgel here at last!"

Six horses, straining and foaming, dragged the cudgel back to the castle, their hoofs sinking into the ground up to their knees. When they eventually got it into the courtyard, Johnny Pea picked it up and spun it on the little finger of his left. It blew up such a wind that all the courtiers' hats flew off their heads and, feathers waving, disappeared over the castle roofs. The ladies' skirts puffed out like balloons and they had to hold them down or they would have taken off, too.

"Enough, enough," cried the king. He called Johnny Pea to him and said, "I can see that you certainly have more strength than is natural, but even so, you must prove one more thing. If it was really you who knocked the cock off the castle roof, you have a sharp eye and steady hand. That is what I'm going to test. In the garden of my other castle, there grows a hazel tree, which has three rare hazel nuts. If from the walls of this castle, you can knock down at least one of those hazels without damaging the tree, you shall become my son-in-law and one day, king of this country. But if you fail, you are a fraud and deceiver and I'll have you executed without mercy."

74

Johnny Pea hesitated when he heard this. Not that he doubted whether he could knock down the hazels, it was not that at all! He wasn't really sure whether he wanted to marry yet. But when he thought it over a little, he came to the conclusion that it probably would be the best thing after all, hadn't he already done enough brave deeds?

He caught up his beloved cudgel, took aim and swoosh! The cudgel flew away, touching only the very tip of the hazel tree and not damaging it in the slightest.

Two hours later a gardener came running from that castle, holding in his palm the three hazel nuts.

"Your Royal Highness!" he gasped, quite out of breath, "someone, who we searched for in vain, has knocked all three of your rare hazel nuts off the tree."

The king patted Johnny on the back, "Well, now I can see you really are the one we are looking for."

He took one of the nuts, broke open the shell and pulled out of it a beautiful star-studded dress.

"My dear, eldest daughter," he said, "this is your wedding gown. Come here and kiss your bridegroom."

The princess pouted her lips. "A bridegroom like that? Never! He'd be gobbled up by the first cat that caught sight of him!"

The king frowned but said nothing. He took the second nut, opened it and pulled out a lovely dress with a pattern of shining moons, "My dear, middle daughter," he said, "this is your wedding gown. Come and kiss your bridegroom." But the princess burst into giggles, "That's meant to be my bridegroom? Never! Why, the cook would throw him into the soup with the peas!"

The king frowned even more darkly, but again he made no comment. He cracked the third nut and pulled out of it a beautiful dress shining like the rays of the sun.

"My dear, youngest daughter, this is your wedding gown. Come here and kiss your bridegroom."

The youngest daughter gazed at Johnny Pea and he gazed at the princess. If this one did not want him either, he would die of shame.

But this princess, looking white and faint, stepped up to him, bent down to the ground and kissed him.

At that moment, Johnny Pea felt as if he was bursting out of his skin. It seemed as if something was lifting him. He looked down and saw to his astonishment that he was standing on long legs! "Give me a mirror," he said.

They brought him a long mirror and he stared into it, Johnny Pea nowhere to be seen! Just a strong young man gazing at him and turning from side to side. It was only when the youngest princess flung her arms around this young man and called him dear, that it dawned on Johnny Pea that he was the man in the mirror. The youngest princess was beside herself with joy, while her two sisters scowled like toads.

It was a really royal wedding. Johnny Pea's parents came too and then stayed on to live in the castle with their son. They sat out in the sunshine, played with their grandchildren and whenever they missed their farming work, there was always some to be found in the fields around the castle.

In time, the old king became tired of ruling and he handed over the throne to his son-in-law. So Johnny Pea became king and reigned happily for the rest of his life.

Brave Sophie

There once was a king who was a great hunter. Not a week went by without the sound of hunting horns echoing in the courtyard, accompanied by the barking of dogs. The walls of the corridors and chambers in the castle were covered with all kinds of precious antlers. The heads of boars, bears, lynxes and bison bared their teeth at the onlooker. The unseeing eyes of eagles, bustards and hawks stared out into the great hall. The king and his huntsmen always returned from the forest with carts piled up high with game.

The years passed and the number of animals in the forest grew less and less. It was high time to do something about it, so the bear, the lord of the forest, called a meeting of the forest animals. The animals met and voiced their complaints against the king.

"He shot my mother when I was still a fawn," one deer lamented. "My sister lost her life at the same time and it was a miracle that I was saved."

A bison was the next to speak. "I am the only one left of all our family," he said in a mournful voice. "When I die, our famous breed will die with me."

And so on, one after the other. All the animals had reason to complain of the king, not one stood up for him. In the end, they agreed that for his cruelty the king deserved no less than death. That was the sentence they passed on him.

The next time the king went hunting, a beautiful stag ran across his path and immediately disappeared into the undergrowth. The king set off after him. The stag appeared again, shook its head to show off its splendid antlers and once more disappeared among the bushes. A wild chase followed during which the king, leaving his huntsmen far behind, flew on and on, he knew not where... Suddenly, the horse found itself sinking in a marsh, the ground gave way and swallowed up both horse and rider.

The huntsmen looked everywhere for the king, they searched every bush, inspected every cave, probed every ravine, but all in vain. They returned home without their king.

Since the king had disappeared, the queen, his wife, took his place on the throne. It was no great loss for the country, rather the opposite, for the queen was not fond of hunting or any other such pastime for that matter, and she devoted her time to government. But it was a great pity that since the king's disappearance, the castle was haunted. The terrified servants fled and so what could the queen do? She had to leave the castle and move into another one. But she was very sorry about this, because she much preferred living in the first castle.

She had it proclaimed throughout the country, that whoever spent the whole of one night in the castle would receive any reward he wished.

This news spread like wildfire and many a darring fellow tried to spend the night in the deserted castle. But when, at midnight, those terrible shrieks, howls, wails and squeals broke the silence, they always took to their heels and were never seen again.

There lived in a little village thereabouts, a girl named Sophie, pretty and well-respected, but as poor as a church mouse. She had a sweetheart and they wanted to get married, but his parents would not hear of it.

"Forget that beggar maid! It's not just that she won't bring you a cow as her dowry, but she hasn't even got a good skirt to her name."

That really was the case, and this made Sophie and her sweetheart very sad. It looked as if fate would part them for ever. Then the girl came to hear of the queen's wish and the reward that she promised. She lost no time and took herself off to the castle. There she explained that she wanted to spend a night in the castle.

"But do you know, dear girl, how many men of all ages have already tried this and failed?" the queen asked her.

"I have heard, Your Highness, but I should like to try all the same. As a reward, I should ask nothing but one cow and one green skirt."

"You can ask for far more," laughed the queen and clapped her hands. Her chambermaid

appeared. "You will take this girl to the haunted castle and give her all she needs," she told him.

But Sophie did not need anything at all. She had brought some spinning with her from home and in the castle she chose a little room with a fireplace to spend the night in. She built a fire in the hearth, sat down on a bench and began to spin, in order to pass the time.

The evening came and night approached. Everything was silent, only the crackling of the fire in the hearth was to be heard. But on the stroke of midnight, there was suddenly such a shrieking, howling, wailing and squealing, it was as if all the animals whose furs, antlers and fangs adorned the benches and walls of the castle had come to life. When the din and uproar was at its height, it suddenly stopped and the sudden silence was broken by the sound of heavy footsteps approaching the room. The steps halted when they came to the door, the door opened by itself and four monsters entered: they had the feet of bears, the jaws of wolves and the horns of bison. On their shoulders, they carried a bier with a dead body. They placed the bier on the ground and left without a word.

Sophie held her breath, she sat and spun, but her hands shook slightly.

Suddenly, the dead man on the bier opened his eyes and sat up. He was richly dressed and he was wearing a crown on his head.

"Spinning, young girl? Spinning?" he spoke to Sophie.

"Spinning, sir, spinning." she replied.

"And do you know who I am?"

"Indeed, I do not, sir."

"Well, I am the king of this country. Would you give the queen a message from me?"

"Gladly, Your Highness," said Sophie.

"Well, tell the queen that my dead body is lying in the seventh valley, at the very edge of the marsh. Tell her to prepare a royal funeral for me and to bury me in the church where my father lies. Also tell her that I forbid hunting horns to disturb me in my sleep."

Having said this, the king lay down on his bier once more and closed his eyes. The monster servants entered the room, picked up the bier and carried it out on their shoulders. Once more the shrieking, howling, wailing and squealing broke the silence, but it

80

soon died down. Then Sophie lay down on the bench and slept quietly until daylight came.

In the morning, she hurried off to see the queen and tell her what she had seen that night and pass on the message the king wanted to send her.

At once, the queen had the king's body brought to her and buried with all the ceremony due to a ruler. In accordance with his wish, she declared that hunting was forbidden.

From that time on, the castle was not haunted, so they could move back to live there.

In return for her brave deed, Sophie received not only a cow and a green skirt, but crimson boots as well and an eiderdown and pillows, in other words, everything a girl must have if she wants to marry, and on top of that she was given a bag of gold ducats.

Then there was nothing to stand in the young couple's way and they could get married. They killed a horned goat, prepared a fine wedding feast and they invited me, too, and gave me wine on a plate and meat in a bottle.

A Father's Advice

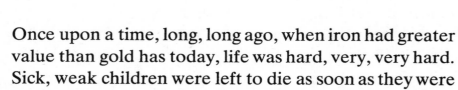

Once upon a time, long, long ago, when iron had greater value than gold has today, life was hard, very, very hard.

Sick, weak children were left to die as soon as they were born so that no bread was wasted on them. Old people, who no longer had the strength to work, were led into the forest and left to the mercy of wild beasts. Such was the custom and such was the Prince's command. Anyone who dared to disobey, risked incurring the cruellest punishment. Yet one such man was found.

One son was so very fond of his father and held him in such high esteem that he decided not to obey the Prince's orders. He dug out a hiding place under the pantry and there he hid his old father from the eyes of the world. The old man came out only at night to get a breath of fresh air and talk to his son.

Several years passed. They were hard years; the country was devastated by war and to add to their misery, there was a terrible drought. The ground did not even give back what the peasants had sown and a tenth went to the Prince's barns. A famine set in.

One day, at the beginning of autumn, the son said to his father, as he was leading him up from his underground hiding-place, "We shall die of hunger, father. Maybe we could get through the winter somehow, but what then, when we have nothing to sow?"

His father bent his head in thought. Then he said, "Do you remember what wonderful barley we had twelve years ago? It stood so high it was taller than the tallest man. We used it to make a new roof for the cottage. Do you remember? You were a young fellow ripe for marrying at the time."

"I remember, father."

"Well, pull the sheaves off the roof and thresh them once more. I think it might be worth your while."

82

His son did as he advised. The neighbours heard the beating of flails and came to see what he was threshing. Surely he could have no more grain left than they had. When they saw that he was flailing the old sheaves and then putting them back on the roof they said, "He's gone out of his mind! It's the hunger that's done it," and they nodded their heads in agreement.

But the peasant threshed a few forgotten grains out of every sheaf. Grain by grain, handful by handful, until he had collected a whole bowlful. He then sowed these grains in the field behind his cottage.

When spring came and summer followed, the fields all over the country were overrun with weeds, but in the young peasant's field, the winter barley stood as high as the cottage roof.

The Prince rode out with his guards to survey his land. It was a sorry sight indeed that met his eyes: people like shadows, peeling the bark off the trees to grind it into powder for a kind of bitter flat-cake. They were scratching among the weeds, searching for wood-sorrel, orach and stinging nettles. In one single field alone, there was barley waving in the breeze, as bright as gold. A true miracle!

The Prince called for the peasant and asked him how it was he had grain for sowing when the country had been afflicted by one catastrophe after another for so many years. The peasant told him the truth, "I pulled the old sheaves off the roof and threshed them once more."

"That idea is worthy of a wise man," said the Prince. "Did you think of it yourself or did someone advise you?"

The peasant hesitated, "Forgive me, sire, if I do not answer that question. I would not dare to lie and I cannot tell the truth."

"But you must tell the truth," said the Prince, frowning gravely, "or your life will be at stake."

"But if I tell you the truth I shall be risking two lives: my own and that of the person who gave me the advice."

"Well, if that is what you fear, I'll give you my word that nothing will happen either to you or to the other person. Now tell me!"

The peasant told him how, out of love for his father, he had disobeyed the Prince's order and not sent his father to his death, but hidden him under his pantry. The peasant also said that, at night, he would talk to him about his work and how his father often gave him good advice. It was thanks to his father's advice that he had gotten that grain last autumn.

The Prince thought hard. That's true, he said to himself: sending old people to their deaths is not only cruel, but it is unwise, too. After all, an old person's wisdom and experience can often be of use to others.

He revoked his cruel command.

Ever since that old people have lived out their lives in peace. While they still have the strength, they help their children and grandchildren, and when they can no longer manage, then their children and grandchildren help them. Or sometimes they don't — it depends on what kind of people they are.

The Girl and the Rooster

A long, long time ago there lived a girl who was not lucky enough to find a husband. All the other girls in the village were already married, not only the rich and pretty ones, but even those who were poorer and uglier than she. This made the girl bad-tempered and she would vent her anger on whatever crossed her path. Most often, this was the rooster. If he came to peck with the hens, she kept chasing him away, as if he was to blame for everything. Go away, you wretched bird!

One day, the girl heard that there was a fortune teller, or perhaps she was even a witch, who could give advice on such matters. The girl summoned up all her courage and set off for the hut in the forest, where this woman was said to live. She told the woman all her troubles and asked whether she could find her a husband of any kind, it didn't even matter if he was lame or cross-eyed.

The fortune teller listened to her attentively and then she knelt down beside her tomcat that was sitting on the stove. She discussed the matter with him in a secret language. The tomcat was black and half his tail was missing. Then, the old woman blew into the ashes, drew something with the little finger of her left hand, nodded her head and said, "Well dear girl, you can set your mind at rest. Tomorrow evening, suitors will appear at your door."

The girl flew home as if she had wings and whitewashed the cottage while her mother baked cakes and roasted meat. The next evening, guests really did arrive at their door and what's more, they came in coaches, no doubt from afar. Smartly dressed like gentlemen, they asked her whether she would not give her hand to their young master, assuring her that she would be well off with him as her husband. The prospective bridegroom smiled, his eyes lit up and he tugged at his black whiskers. The girl liked him at first sight and he liked her.

Well, the matter was quickly settled, the guests sat down at the table and ate, sang and made merry. By chance the bridegroom dropped his fork on the floor... The girl bent down to pick it up — and what did she see! Instead of feet the bridegroom had hoofs! She realized at once what it meant, but she made no sign, except for turning very pale, because she knew what awaited her. She quickly began racking her brains to find some way out. Then she remembered the rooster. If only he would crow all of a sudden, these guests would fall back to hell.

The girl secretly broke off a piece of cake and slipped it into her pocket. Then she got up from the table, went out into the courtyard and made straight for the henhouse. She opened the door of the henhouse and begged,

Crow, rooster, please crow
Or to hell, I shall go!

But the rooster was still feeling offended.

"When you fed the hens, you kept me at bay,
You shooed and cursed and chased me away."

But the girl begged him,

You'll live like a king,
You can wish anything.
But crow, rooster, crow,
Or to hell, I must go!

Then she gave him a piece of the wedding cake.

She begged so hard, the rooster gave in and crowed at the top of his voice, even though it was still long before midnight.

No sooner had his crowing rung out, the devilish guests disappeared in a flash. All that remained was the smell you find in a blacksmith's forge.

Of course the girl was glad to have had such a lucky escape, but the devils were angry, and even ashamed, that the wedding should have ended like that. They decided they would take revenge by flooding the village.

They began to carry rocks into the narrow valley to make a dam across the stream. They had built up quite a pile of rocks by the break of dawn, but as soon as the rooster crowed, it collapsed. They tried the next night, but the same thing happened: what they had built only collapsed again when the rooster crowed at daybreak. So it happened again and again.

In the end, they realized that their plan of revenge was not going to succeed, so they gave up trying.

A short time later the girl did get married after all. Her husband did not have sparkling eyes, nor a beautiful moustache, but he did have real sturdy legs and no hoofs. He made a good husband and loving father.

The girl took the rooster with her to her new home. She looked after him very well and would never allow anyone to harm him, so in the end he died of ripe old age.

Princess Prattella

There was once a king and he had one daughter, Princess Prattella. At first, he was very sorry that he had no son to inherit his throne, but later he comforted himself with the thought that Prattella would grow up, get married and bring a young king to the palace. If only she would make a good choice!

Time passed quickly, Princess Prattella grew more charming and more beautiful every day. Even before she reached her sixteenth birthday, the palace became a meeting place for all kinds of princes from all over the world. Their days were filled with fun and laughter.

"The prince from the seventh kingdom is very charming," Princess Prattella prattled on to the old gardener when, as was her custom, she came to the greenhouse for a rose. "Everything he says is so funny, such a joker, hahahahaha! And the crown prince from the twenty-fifth kingdom has a transparent honey-coloured stone with a drop of water inside, really! It flows along a stone path, beautiful! But the most exceptional prince of them all, is the king from the thirty-third kingdom, because he has a really strong rooster. He lets his rooster out in the courtyard and ties a huge oak log to its leg. And what do you think this rooster does? It walks up and down as if the log was as light as a feather! It must be the strongest rooster in the world! The king said he'd give it to me if I chose him to be my husband."

The gardener smiled, but it was a sad smile.

"I'm sure Your Highness will make the right choice."

"Of course I will. I'll probably choose the rooster, I mean, the king with the rooster. Instead of the log, I'll harness it to my coach, or to my sledge in the winter. The whole world will gasp in amazement when they see me drawn along by a rooster. I'll give you a ride sometime, too, at least from the garden to the gates." She prattled on, darting here and there among the rose bushes and the gardener listened to her in silence and nodded his head gravely.

When he had seen her off, he returned to his work. Suddenly, he noticed something caught on a thorn of a rose bush. It was the princess's silken scarf.

Fate had sent it to him!

He pulled the scarf off the bush and took it to a corner of the greenhouse. There he plucked a four-leaved clover and sewed it into the edge of the scarf. A four-leaved clover, just in case there is anyone who doesn't know, has a special power: it opens people's eyes, so that they can see through every fraud and deceit to the very heart.

The next day, the gardener returned the scarf to the princess and in his heart, he wished, "May this four-leaved clover help you to choose the right husband, our little prattling Prattella."

Just that day, the king from the thirty-third kingdom had decided to ask for Prattella's hand in marriage. He would use the moment when the princess would be admiring the strength of his rooster. He brought the cage from his room, let the rooster out and fixed the oak log to his leg so that it would walk up and down with it.

Everyone in the palace had seen this at least once, but even so, they clapped their hands and gasped in admiration, their eyes almost popping out of their heads. Princess Prattella also opened her eyes wide, but she did not gasp, she only exclaimed in ridicule, "Can't you all see that it isn't a log it's pulling, but an ordinary piece of straw?'' She laughed and laughed, her laughter was so catching that very soon all the others were in fits of laughter as well. That laughter opened their eyes, too: just imagine, it really was an ordinary piece of straw, an ordinary rooster, an ordinary fraud! They laughed and were delighted that of all Prattella's suitors, it should be this one that she should dismiss, because he had seemed to be their greatest rival.

But the king from the thirty-third kingdom was not in a mood for laughter at all. Not only had his plan been foiled, but he had become a target of ridicule. He could not leave it at that!

He stepped up to Prattella, who was still laughing, gave her a piercing glare which sent a shiver down her back, blew in her face and left without a word. A giddy feeling came over Prattella and she had to sit down. Her eyelids felt heavy and she had to close them. Her mind went hazy and she fell into a deep, deep sleep.

She slept one day, she slept two days, she slept three days, she slept the whole week. The princes left the castle one by one and all kinds of doctors, charlatans and herbalists took their place.

One decided to cure the princess by bringing a whole orchestra, drums and all, into her bed chamber. The orchestra blared, clashed and banged, but the princess just slept and slept, smiling sweetly in her sleep.

The second doctor arranged around her bed three dozen alarm

clocks. Every half hour the clocks shattered the silence with such an ear-splitting brrr-trrr-drrr that all the pictures in the palace fell off the wall. But the princess just slept and slept, smiling sweetly in her sleep.

They tried all kinds of other things as well, but all in vain.

Finally, the king sent out a proclamation, that whoever woke up the princess, would receive her hand in marriage.

This news spread like wildfire to the farthest corners and the most out-of-the-way places in the realm. It even reached Timothy, a charcoal burner, who lived with his young wife, somewhere a long way off in the middle of the forest.

Timothy could not put the idea of the sleeping princess out of his mind. He remembered something his father had told him as they were walking through the forest one day when he was still a child. The forest was so terribly deep that it was dark, damp and totally deaf. His father had pointed to an old wil-low and said, "That willow has never heard the sound of water or a rooster crowing. A willow like that has great power, remember that my son."

Timothy had listened carefully and had intended to tell his own son one day before he died. But as he had never made use of the secret, he had nearly forgotten about it. At this moment, it came into his mind, as if his father was now saying. "That willow has ne-ver heard the sound of water or a rooster crowing. A willow like that has great power, remember that, my son."

"Has it the power to wake up a sleeping princess?" Timothy wondered. Perhaps he should try. Of course, he did not want the princess for his wife, he was married already. Anyway, what kind of marriage would that be? A charcoal burner and a princess! Or would the princess come to live in a charcoal burner's humble cottage? The very thought of it! Even so, he would try to see whether he could wake her up from that strange sleep.

Timothy set out into that deep forest. He went on and on, though there was no path, or track. He also waded through snow up to his waist. It took an enormous effort to push his way through to that willow, and when he reached it, he was astonished how very ordinary it looked. Timothy broke off a slender branch and felt something sticky on his fingers, sap! Now? In the middle of winter? he wondered. He tapped the branch with the handle of his knife, hollowed it out to make a whistle and put it to his lips. Just imagine — no sooner had he blown the first notes, that the snow began to melt, the trees burst into bud, the first snowdrops peeped out and a bird broke into song. Everything around him was waking up. Timothy strode off straight through the forest. As he went, he whistled and as he whistled the water in the rivers stirred to life, the grass in the meadows turned green, the breeze began to dance in the bushes. He soon found himself in front of the royal palace and asked to see the king.

"It's like this," Timothy told the king, "I've come to see whether I can wake up her royal highness, your daughter." At once, the king led him to the room, where Princess Prattella was sleeping on a silken bed and smiling a sweet smile in her sleep.

Timothy began to play on his magic whistle. At first, the princess just murmured in her sleep as if in answer to somebody's call. But soon she turned over on her side, stretched her arms, rubbed her eyes and then opened them, smiling happily, "Oh, how well I have slept!"

She jumped out of bed and flung her arms around her father, then she turned to Timothy and embraced him, too. His peasant's clothing did not mislead her. After all, she was wearing her silken scarf with the four-leaved clover, with the help of which, she could see deep into his very heart.

The king was not very pleased by the appearance of this bridegroom, but a promise is a promise.

"You have done what was required of you," he said, "and I will keep my promise. The wedding can take place in three days' time."

"What wedding?" the charcoal burner exclaimed in alarm.

"Yours and Princess Prattella's, of course."

"But I'm already married, sire," Timothy explained. "I came to help the Princess just out of good will, because I felt sorry for her. Let her choose someone else to be her husband, someone more fitting for a life of royal luxury." He looked at Prattella affectionately, for she was lovely. She looked at Timothy with admiration, because he was a strong, well-built man and an honest spirit shined in his eyes.

"Well, at least take something as a reminder of me."

"A reminder?" Timothy gazed around the beautiful palace: marble, carpets, inlaid furniture, and gold goblets. What use would they be to him?

"Everything here is so big and heavy, there isn't room for it in my cottage."

"Well, you know what?" Prattella had an idea. "I'll give you this scarf." She pulled from her belt the silk scarf with the four-leaved clover sewn in the hem.

"Thank you, Princess, I'll take that gladly," Timothy said happily, folding up the scarf and putting it into the inner pocket of his peasant's smock, where he always kept the most precious things he had.

With a feeling of satisfaction, he set off for his cottage in the middle of the forest.

But it seemed that Prattella had given away her eyes when she gave away her scarf. She could no longer see into anyone's heart, she had lost that gift once and for all and we know why.

Princes from all over the world streamed into the palace, hoping to win the princess' favor. At last, Prattella chose the prince that wore a coat with gilt buttons embossed with a hawk's head, just because the hawk's head looked so true-to-life.

Johnny Linden-Log

In a little house, on the bank of a stream, there lived a man and his wife. They had no children and that made them very sad. One day the woman said to her husband, "Listen. We have no children, but, at least, carve me one out of wood."

The man happened to have a little time, so he chose a smooth linden log and carved a boy out of it. It was a handsome boy, he looked wise and brave. He had only one fault, he was not alive. But even so, the wife pressed him to her heart, laid him gently in a cradle and rocked him, singing this song to him:

> *Sleep, sleep, my little son,*
> *Then wake and play and run,*
> *You're sure to know the art*
> *Of gladdening my sad heart.*

She sang it once and the wooden boy blinked his eyes. She sang it again and the wooden boy waved his arms. She sang it for a third time and the wooden boy jumped out of his cradle. He flung his arms around his mother and father and cried, "I'm awake! I'll play and run and gladden your sad hearts!"

The man and his wife were overcome with joy, they brought out all the food they had and prepared a feast to welcome their son into the world. As he had been made out of a log, they called him Johnny Linden-log.

Johnny Linden-log grew and grew. He ran around and played. He was happiest when he could play by the stream. His father made him a little boat and he sailed up and down, always catching a lot of fish. In this way, he helped his father to make a living for the family. His mother used to bring him his lunch there. Whenever she came to the bank of the stream, she sang in a sweet voice,

Come here, my little son,
Enough work you have done,
You surely know the art
Of gladdening your mother's heart.

No matter how far away he was, Johnny always heard this song and sailed up in his boat, ate his lunch, talked happily with his mother and then set off again to catch more fish.

Thus they lived in peace, without the slightest suspicion that disaster lay in store for them.

In the dense forest, on the other side of the stream, there lived a witch. Many a time she had listened when Johnny's mother called him and she had learned her song. One day, at noon, she crept up to the bank of the stream and sang,

Come here, my little son,
Enough work you have done,
You sure do know the art
Of gladdening your mother's heart.

Johnny Linden-log heard her with surprise: her voice was somehow different, rather hoarse, but the song was his mother's. Maybe his mother had caught a cold and was losing her voice. He

mustn't keep her waiting long. He swiftly turned the boat around and sailed in the direction of the song. But he had hardly stepped out onto the bank when the witch jumped out from behind a bush, seized the boy and dragged him off to her hut in the middle of the deep forest. She shut him up in the pantry and went to stoke up the fire, so that she could roast Johnny for her supper.

Poor boy, he knew that he was in terrible danger, but he did not panic. He looked around the pantry to see if there was any way of escape. As he was searching, he came across a mouse-hole in one corner. That was at least something!

He began to pick away at the wall around the hole. He broke his nails and made his fingers bleed before he managed to make it big enough to crawl through. Just as he slipped out of the pantry, the witch stepped in! She had come for him because the fire under the stove was now blazing hot.

But the pantry was empty, with a hole gaping wide in the wall. At once she realized what had happened and she flew out of the house after Johnny. Before long, she was on his heels, a few strides more and she would catch him up!

At this moment, Johnny Linden-log caught sight of a high

oak-tree, its branches stretching up into the clouds. He began to scramble up the oak, as quick as a squirrel. He was at the top in no time. There he sat astride a branch and waited to see what would happen next.

The witch was furious, she almost burnt up with rage: the boy was there, so near and yet so far. She had long forgotten how to climb trees.

She went back to the hut and fetched three axes. Then she set to work to fell the tree.

Poor Johnny knew how this must end. But just then he noticed a flock of wild geese in the sky. He called to them, begging for help:

> *Dear geese, wild geese, fly over here,*
> *And take me on your wings.*
> *Carry me off, over hill, over dale*
> *To where my mother sings.*
> *We'll give you seed, we'll give you corn,*
> *We'll feast you better than kings.*

But the geese said, "There's another flock behind us. They can take you."

Just at that moment, the witch broke the first axe and the oak tree rocked. Johnny Linden-log looked desperately around to see if anyone could save him from disaster. Then he caught sight of a second flock of geese, flying in his direction. He called out to them pitifully:

> *Dear geese, wild geese, fly over here,*
> *And take me on your wings.*
> *Carry me off, over hill, over dale*
> *To where my mother sings.*
> *We'll give you seed, we'll give you corn,*
> *We'll feast you better than kings.*

But the geese said to him, "There's one more goose flying behind us, let her take you!"

Just then, the witch broke the second axe and the oak rocked dangerously. It very nearly toppled to the ground.

At that moment, a lonely old goose flew right over the top branches of the oak. Johnny Linden-log called out to her in a despairing voice,

Dear goose, wild goose, fly over here,
And take me on your wings.
Carry me off, over hill, over dale
To where my mother sings.
We'll give you seed, we'll give you corn,
We'll feast you better than kings.

The goose said to him, "Jump on to my back!"

Johnny Linden-log jumped astride her and at that very moment, the giant oak tree crashed to the ground.

The old goose flew over that deep, dark forest, flew over the stream and landed on the roof of Johnny's house. Johnny Linden-log looked down the chimney into the room and saw that his mother and father were sitting at lunch, but they were not eating. They were weeping for their lost son, their tears dropping into their plates. Then Johnny called out, "Don't cry, dear mother and father, I'm here!"

Their joy cannot be described in words. All three wept, but now from happiness. Even the old goose who had saved Johnny Linden-log quietly shed a tear or two. She did not fly on, she stayed at the house by the side of the stream and never felt lonely again.

The Two Sisters

Once upon a time, in a far distant country, where they raked up water and bound sand in sheaves, there lived a man and his wife with their two girls. One was the man's daughter and the other, his wife's. The husband was fond of both girls, but his wife loved only her own daughter. She hated her step-daughter and kept chasing her out of the house. What could the poor girl do? With a heavy heart, she set out into the world.

She walked on and on until she came to a stove that was full of red-hot coals.

"Good day, stove," the girl greeted it.

"Good day to you, young girl. Where are you going?"

"I'm going to look for work as a servant girl."

"Would you do me a service, too?"

"I'd be very glad to."

"Well, rake these coals out of me, they're quite burning me up."

The girl took the poker and raked the coals out of the stove.

The stove sighed in relief and said, "You are a good girl, thank you."

The girl came to a spring and it was quite blocked up with mud.

"Good day, spring!" she greeted it.

"Good day to you, young girl. Where are you going?"

"I'm going to look for work as a servant girl."

"Would you do me a service, too?"

"I'd be very glad to."

"Then clear this mud out of me, no one has cleaned me for such a long time."

The girl cleaned the mud out of the spring and went on her way.

She walked and walked until she came to an apple tree. Its branches were heavy with apples.

"Good day, apple tree," she greeted it.

"Good day to you, young girl. Where are you going?"

"I'm going to look for work as a servant girl."

"Would you do me a service, too?"

"I'd be very glad to, apple tree."

"Well, shake these apples off me, I can't hold them any longer."

The girl scrambled up the apple tree, shook it, and the apples came tumbling down on the ground.

She went on until she came to a coach, which was harnessed to four horses.

"Good day, horses," she greeted them.

"Good day to you too, young girl. Where are you going?"

"I'm going to look for work as a servant girl."

"Would you do us a service, too?"

"I'd be very glad to, horses."

"Well, comb us, it's so long since anyone took care of us."

The girl combed them until they shone. Then she went on her way.

She walked on and on until she came to a cottage where an old man lived.

"Good day, old man," she greeted him.

"Good day to you, young girl. Where are you going?"

"I'm looking for work as a servant girl, do you know of any?"

"You can serve me," said the old man. "All you have to do is keep my house in order and look after my cat and dog. I am going on a journey and I shall return in a year's time."

The old man led the girl into his pantry and showed her where he kept the lentils, peas and other food.

"Cook this and live on it for the coming year," he told her and departed.

The girl was left with the man's cat and dog. She brushed them nicely, then tidied up the cottage, cooked the lunch and they all ate their fill. So it went on, day after day; they lived contentedly and the year passed in no time.

When the old man was approaching the house, the cat and dog ran out to meet him.

"Well, how did the girl look after you?" asked the old man.

"Very well," they replied. "If only we always had someone who looked after us so well!"

The old man nodded his head in satisfaction. When he arrived at the cottage, he led the girl into a room which was full of all kinds of chests and coffers and said, "Choose any one you like as your reward for good service."

The girl gazed at the chests and thought to herself, "I can't take a large one, I couldn't carry it far." So she chose the smallest one that fit under her arm.

"Don't open it until you get home," the old man said to her. The girl thanked him, said goodbye to the old man, the cat and the dog and set off for home.

She walked on and on. The little chest, no matter how small it was, was heavy for her, it pressed uncomfortably into her side. The girl

began to wonder whether she would have to open it and throw something out of it so she could walk more easily.

But at that moment, a coach came clattering up drawn by four prancing horses, "Step up into the coach, young girl, we will take you home," they said.

She stepped up into the coach and the horses flew off as if they had wings.

They came to the apple tree. The apple tree bent down over the coach and handed the girl three beautiful apples. What a wonderful taste they had!

The horses galloped on, in no time they were at the spring. The spring sparkled and handed the girl a glass of fresh water. Ah! that was good!

The horses flew on and on and they came to the stove.

"Taste my cake, young girl," said the stove and offered her a piece of delicious, warm cake. The girl ate her fill and then the horses took her home.

She put the chest down on the table and opened it. Her eyes met the glitter of gold coins and precious stones, some were as green as grass, others as blue as the sky and others as red as blood.

That very day, messengers came to ask for the step-daughter's hand in marriage to a young handsome man. He was poor, it's true, but what did that matter. They sold a precious stone and bought a cottage together with a stable. They sold another gem and bought oxen and a cow to put in the stable. They sold a third stone and bought a field and a plough for the oxen. They sold a fourth stone and bought a meadow for the cow, as well as a rake and a scythe. They still had enough to buy plates and dishes and a mirror, boots, a fur coat and a silken scarf.

At the sight of all this, the stepmother and her daughter were eaten up with envy.

"How did you come by such wealth?" they asked.

The step-daughter told them the truth, "There is an old man living in such and such a place and I worked as a servant girl for him."

The stepmother's daughter set out to look for the man and work as his servant.

She went on and on until she came to the stove. But she didn't greet it or even take any notice of it at all for that matter.

"Young girl," said the stove, "would you take these coals out of me? They're quite burning me up!"

"I will not!" said the girl. "I might burn holes in my dress!"

She went on until she came to the spring.

"Young girl," said the spring, "would you clear this mud out of me? It's so long since anyone cleaned me out."

"The very idea!" retorted the girl. "I'd get my clothes wet!"

She went on until she came to the apple tree. The apple tree begged her, "Young girl, shake these apples off me, I can't hold them any longer."

"Who do you think you are to ask such a thing!" she answered huffily. I'd only tear my dress!"

She went on until she came to the horses. "Stop a moment and comb us," begged the horses. "It's so long since anyone took care of us!"

"Whatever will you think of next! I'd only dirty my dress!"

Soon she came to the cottage where the old man lived.

"Good day," she greeted him. "Was it in your house that my sister served?"

"Yes, it was," said the old man.

"Would you take me into your service, too?"

"Yes, I'll take you, because I am just about to leave and there is no one to look after my cat and dog."

He showed the girl where he kept the lentils, peas and other food and went away for a whole year.

The girl was left with the cat and the dog, but she did not take good care of them at all. She cooked for herself, and she always ate well, but all she gave the cat and dog was the dirty pots and pans to lick.

A year passed, the old man was coming home. The cat and dog ran out to meet him and he asked them, "Well, how did the girl look after you?"

"Very badly. We were hungry for most of the time."

The old man said nothing, just nodded his head. When he arrived at his cottage, he led the girl into the room with the chests and coffers.

"Your time has come," he told her, "choose a reward for your service."

This was the moment she had been waiting for. She chose a large chest, lifted it up on to her shoulder and set off for home.

She walked on and on, the chest getting heavier every step she took. When she reached the horses harnessed to the coach she begged them, "Would you drive me home?"

"We are not combed, we would dirty your dress," said the horses. They kicked up their hoofs and disappeared from view.

"Oh, why didn't I comb them!" sighed the girl.

104

She went on, her knees giving way under her. Ah, there was the apple tree. She would ask for an apple, perhaps that would give her strength.

But the branches of the apple tree hung cracked and bare, they had broken under the weight of the fruit.

"Oh, why didn't I shake the apples off it!" the girl thought with regret.

She dragged herself on, soon she would be at the spring and there she could get a drink of water at least.

But the spring was full of mud, not a drop of water could it offer.

"Oh, why didn't I clean it out!" the girl lamented.

Making a last effort, the girl forced herself to go on, soon she would come to the stove, at least she could ask it for a piece of cake.

But the stove was full of holes that the red-hot coals had made in it and the cake was burnt to ashes.

"Oh, why didn't I rake out the coals!" the girl burst into tears.

It was almost more than she could do to drag herself home. Her mother caught sight of her from the window and ran to meet her. "Look, look everyone, see what my daughter has earned for her services, a chest full of gems!"

They were but a few steps from each other when the girl's legs gave way under her and the chest slipped off her shoulder. The lid was torn off and something began to crawl out from underneath it; snakes, frogs and all kinds of other horrible beasts.

"Beautiful gems indeed!" people laughed. "Some of them crawl and others leap."

The girl fled into the cottage and it was a long, long time before she dared show herself in public. She never got married either, no young man wanted her. "What that one?" they all laughed. "Why she hatches snakes in her chest!"

The Tree that Adorns All,
the Water that Revives All,
and the Bird that Reveals All

A young king once went out for a walk and came across a lonely cottage. He sat down on the bench outside to rest and as he sat, the sound of voices came to his ears. He looked through the window and saw three girls sitting on a bench at a wheel spinning.

"Who knows who we'll marry," said one. "Or whether we will end up as old maids."

"If I could choose," said the eldest, "I would choose the royal cook to be my husband. That would be the life for me! Every day my husband would bring me some titbit or other from the royal kitchens."

"And if I could choose," said the middle daughter, "I would choose the royal chamberlain. I would live like a lady, moving in and out of the royal chamber, looking at the royal robes."

"And if I could choose," said the youngest of them, "I should choose his highness, our king. I would love him and in time, we would have children — two boys and a girl. And they would be as healthy as water, as busy as bees and as rich as the earth."

The older sisters began to pout and grumble that the youngest had chosen the king so she could boss them around. Just at that moment, the door opened and the very person they had been talking about, the young king himself, stepped in. He bowed to them politely and said, "I heard what you wished, young ladies, and because I like you, I will see to it that your wishes come true. The eldest of you shall marry the royal cook, the next the royal chamberlain and the youngest will become my wife and the queen of this country."

106

Very soon this happened, the three weddings took place and the three sisters began to live in the royal palace.

They had every reason to be satisfied now their dreams had come true, but the two elder sisters were green with envy, they could not bear the thought of their younger sister being queen.

Unhappily, the country was attacked by a neighboring ruler and so the young king had to go into battle. Before he left, he asked the cook and the chamberlain's wives to look after the queen, who was soon to bear a child, and he gave orders that no one else was to be allowed near her.

The time came when the queen gave birth to a beautiful boy. But the queen's sisters snatched the little boy away and put a puppy in his place. They did it so cleverly that no one in the palace, not even the queen herself, noticed what they had done. They put the baby into a basket and let it float off down the river. Then they wrote to the king at the battlefield to tell that the queen had given birth, not to a child, but to a puppy, and that everyone felt very sorry for the king. The king was terribly sad, but nevertheless, he wrote that they should take great care of the queen and her puppy. When he eventually came home and saw that his wife looked sad, but even more beautiful than before, he forgave her everything and they once more lived together as a happy couple should.

Time passed and the queen was due to give birth to a second child, and again the king had to depart to the battlefield. He entrusted his 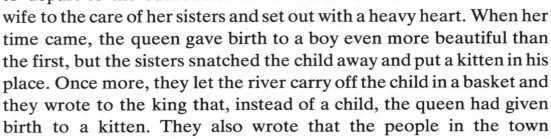 wife to the care of her sisters and set out with a heavy heart. When her time came, the queen gave birth to a boy even more beautiful than the first, but the sisters snatched the child away and put a kitten in his place. Once more, they let the river carry off the child in a basket and they wrote to the king that, instead of a child, the queen had given birth to a kitten. They also wrote that the people in the town considered him, the king, as more an object of ridicule than sympathy. This letter made the king extremely unhappy and he wrote that he would soon be returning and would look into the matter. Until that time, they should take care of the queen and her kitten.

When he returned from battle and saw his wife twice as sad, but twice as beautiful, he once more forgave her everything and they lived together as a loving couple should.

But bad luck usually comes in threes.

The queen was to give birth for the third time and again, the king had to go into battle. He entrusted his wife to the care of her sisters and sadly left home.

The time came and the queen gave birth to a lovely little girl. But her sisters again snatched the child away, putting a piece of rotten wood in its place.

They hid the child in a basket and let it float off down the river, at the mercy of the waters. Then they wrote to the king to tell him that his wife had given birth, not to a child, but to a piece of rotten wood. The people in the town were up in arms that the queen should bring such shame on the royal house and on the whole of the country, and everyone thought she must be a witch.

The king was seized with anger for his young wife and even he was now ready to believe that there must be black magic involved. So when he returned home, he sentenced the queen to imprisonment for life. He had a dungeon dug out for her in front of the church, with a single opening covered by a grating and he sent out a command that everyone who went that way should spit on her through that opening. So it was. For years and years, the queen languished in prison and everyone who went past had to spit on her. The people thought it was just punishment for a woman who gave birth to strange beasts instead of children.

Meanwhile the queen's sons grew into fine young men and their sister into a young maiden as lovely as a flower. When their mother's sisters threw them into the water, the river did not harm them. It carefully passed them from wave to wave until it had carried them to one large garden. The garden belonged to a man who did not have any children of his own, he was only too happy when the river swept two boys and then a girl up onto the bank. He brought up all three as best he could and they were lovely children, as healthy as water and as busy as bees. When they were big enough, they helped their foster father in the garden, which not only provided them with food, but also filled their hearts with beauty. Travellers, who stopped to rest in the shade of its trees, always used to say that there was no garden to compare with it. When they saw the three handsome foundlings, they thought to themselves, who knows whether the children lend beauty to the garden or the garden lends beauty to them?

One day an old woman was hobbling past. She stopped beside the garden and even went inside to rest for a while. She looked all around and was lost in admiration.

"It is a lovely garden, really beautiful," she said, "but it could be

even more beautiful. It could be the most beautiful garden in the world if only it had three magic things."

"What magic things?" asked the gardener and the children the river had brought him.

"Well, somewhere in the world is a tree that adorns all, from under whose roots there springs water that revives all and in its branches there lives a bird that reveals all."

"I shall go to find those things and bring them to our garden," said the elder brother. "Please just tell me which way I should go."

The old woman stretched out her hand, picked an apple from a tree and handed it to him. It would show him the path, she said. Then she went on her way.

The elder brother wove a garland of leaves and gave it to his younger brother with the words, "While this garland is fresh and green, I am alive and well. But if it should wilt, that will be a sign that my life has wilted too and then, dear brother, hurry to my rescue."

The young man leapt up on his horse, threw the apple in front of him and followed it wherever it went. The apple came to a halt in front of a hill and there at the foot of the slope, lay an old man. His beard was twice as long as himself and his fingernails reached down to his toes.

"A good day to you, Mr. Longbeard."

"Welcome, young prince," the old man replied.

"If I am a prince, I know nothing about it. The river brought me and a gardener is both a guardian and father to me. I have set out into the world in search of three magic things: a tree that adorns all, water that revives all and a bird that reveals all. Could you advise me, sir, which way to go?"

"You have set yourself a difficult task, young prince," said Longbeard, "and I really don't know whether you will succeed. For these things are to be found in an enchanted castle, and whoever wants to get there must not look around even once, no matter what happens. If he looks back, be it but once, that will be the end of him."

"Well, I shall take great care," said the young man and, thanking him for his advice, went on his way. Very soon he caught sight of a castle on the top of a hill. It was only one valley away. But as he went on, snakes began to hiss at him, wolves, bears and all kinds of other beasts leapt out at him. He had to hold his sword ready all the time. What was worse, voices called to him from all sides, sometimes lovingly, sometimes angrily, sometimes with a note of warning.

"Listen to good advice, go back home while there is still time!"

"You are lost for ever, you will become a black stone!"

"Those who listen and obey, do not die. Save your soul while there is still time!" The voices were followed by the sound of trees crashing to the ground and rolling down the slopes in his direction. The young man very nearly looked around to see

which way he should jump, but he just managed to control himself as Longbeard's words flashed through his mind: "Don't look around even once, no matter what happens." In this way, he passed through more than half the valley, when a voice suddenly came from behind him, a voice more loving and kind than he had ever heard, but which he had dreamed of many a time: a voice such as his mother would have, if only he had a mother.

"What are you doing here, my son?"

This was too much for the young man, he looked around and at that very moment, he was changed into a black stone.

Back at home, his brother and sister kept a close watch on the garland. For two days it was fresh and green, until, on the third day, it suddenly wilted.

"It seems our brother can't manage without me," said the younger son, "I must go to rescue him without delay."

He got ready, but before he left, he wove a garland of leaves and gave it to his sister, so that she would know how he was. Then he leapt astride his horse and set off, following his brother's trail. He came to the hill at the foot of which the old man lay, his beard twice as long as himself and his nails reaching down to his toes.

"Good health to you, Mr. Longbeard," he greeted him.

"Good health to you, too, young prince."

"If I am a prince, I know nothing about it. I am a gardener's ward, the river brought me to him. Could you tell me, sir, whether my brother has passed this way? He was looking for three magic things:

a tree that adorns all, water that revives all and a bird that reveals all."

"Yes, indeed, he did go this way and I advised him what to do, but he did not keep to my advice. No wonder, it is a hard task and no one has yet succeeded." He told the young man what had happened to his brother and how he could get into the castle where the three magic things were to be found.

The young man thanked him for his advice and went on. He, too, came to that valley and fought his way through all kinds of snakes, wolves, bears and other beasts, all kinds of pleas and threats filling his ears, but he strode straight on, looking neither to the right, nor to the left. When he was more than half way through the valley, his eyes fell on a pile of stones, and among them he recognized his brother, changed into a black rock. Tears came into the young man's eyes and he cried out, "Oh, my poor brother!"

From behind him came a voice, "Don't mourn for me, dear brother, I am alive!"

The young man swung around in joy to embrace his brother and in the same instant, he turned into a black stone.

At home, his sister kept looking at the garland. For two days it was fresh and green, but on the third day, it suddenly wilted, as if blighted by frost.

"Well, who would have thought it!" she mused to herself. "Neither of them can manage without my help." So she hurriedly got ready to go to their aid, although the gardener pleaded with her to stay at home, because she was sure to perish there too. The girl would not listen, she saddled her horse and off she galloped! Very soon she reached the hill at the foot of which the old man lay, his beard twice as long as himself and nails down to his toes.

"Good day to you, Mr. Longbeard," she greeted him.

"Good day to you, princess," Longbeard replied.

"If I am a princess, I know nothing about it. I have lived all my life in a gardener's house. The river brought me there. Now I am looking for my two brothers, who went in search of three magic things: a tree which adorns all, water that revives all and a bird which reveals all. But you have such a long beard and such long nails that no doubt you can't get up because of them."

She took a pair of scissors out of her bundle and cut off his nails and beard. The old man gave a sigh of relief, as if a heavy burden had fallen from him and he immediately raised himself from the ground.

"You have done me a great service, dear princess. For thousands of years I have lain here but the strength of my beard has prevented me from dying. You have broken the spell laid on me. At last, the earth will receive me. Bury me here and then go after your brothers." Then he told her how and what she should do and warned her, for heavens' sake, not to turn around even once, no matter what happened. He gave her a hair from his beard, telling her that if she touched the gates of the enchanted castle with it, they would fly open.

When he had finished telling her all she needed to know, he closed his eyes and died. She dug out as good a grave as she could and buried him in it. Then she went on her way.

She, too, came to that valley, on the other side of which stood the castle on the top of a hill. Snakes and all kinds of other beasts began to jump out at her as if to tear her to pieces, but she took no notice of them, just walking on through the valley. All kinds of voices called to her, sometimes as if from afar, sometimes as if hissing right in her ear, "Death is walking behind you, go back, you stupid girl!"

She ignored them, looking neither to the right nor to the left. When she was more than halfway through the valley, she caught sight of her two brothers, turned to stone. She stopped in front of them, tears running down her cheeks. At that moment, she heard their voices behind her, "Don't mourn for us, sister, we are alive and well!"

Their sister's heart leapt for joy and she was just about to swing around when she stopped and said, "If you are alive and well, then come here, because I must not look around."

She waited a while to see if they would come and when they did not, she knew for certain that it had been a trick. So she went on until she came to that castle. She touched the gates with the hair from the old man's beard, they flew open and she stepped inside.

The very first thing to meet her eyes was a tree such as no one has ever seen before. Every leaf was of a different colour and when the breeze blew there came a harmonious chorus of sounds, as if all the leaves were playing different instruments and together making a beautiful magic melody such as no one had ever heard before.

On that tree, on the lowest branch, hung a golden cage in which a little bird hopped up and down.

"You must be the bird that reveals all," the girl spoke to it. "Well, tell me, please, what should I do to bring my brothers back to life?"

The bird twittered as if playing on a silver string, "Draw water of life that bubbles and sparkles and sprinkle it over your brothers to break that black spell."

The girl looked around and caught sight of a spring at the foot of the tree. The water was bubbling and sparkling, leaping, foaming and spraying up into the air. She filled a jug with it and ran back to the valley. She sprinkled the black rocks that were her brothers and all the others, too, and one by one they turned into people, who embraced the girl and thanked her for setting them free.

She and her brothers returned to the castle once more. There they broke a branch off the tree that adorns all, filled a jug with water that revives all and from the lowest branch of the tree, they took the golden cage with the bird that reveals all. Then they set off for home. Once there, they planted the branch in the middle of the garden and the branch put out roots and soon grew into a tall tree. Every leaf was of a different colour and when the breeze blew it rustled a magically beautiful melody. At the sound of the music, everything in the garden grew as if by magic. The grass was greener, the roses more fragrant, the fruit more juicy, and even the morning dew was fresher and brighter.

The fame of this garden spread far and wide. People came to see the tree that adorns all and they listened to its music with baited breath. They gazed in admiration at the water that bubbled and sparkled, foamed and leapt and sprayed up into the air, and they gasped in wonder at the little bird who knew what no one else knew.

The king also came to hear of these wonders and decided that he should go to see them for himself. His sisters-in-law tried in vain to persuade him not to go. What was the point of wearing oneself out going so far, they said. Everyone knew that the most beautiful garden in the world was his own royal garden, even though it had no magic in it.

The king did not let himself be put off. He got into his coach and went.

When he came to that garden, his own three children welcomed him and led him to the miraculous tree, but, of course, they did not know him for what he was, nor he them. The king thought to himself, "How charming they are, healthy as water, busy as bees and as rich as the earth. He could not take his eyes off these three young people. For him, they were an even greater miracle than the three magic things. He felt so happy in their company, he was sorry to leave. In the end, he said, "Well, I have been your guest, and now you must come to the royal town to visit me."

The brothers and sister promised and a few days later, a coach arrived to take them there. When they came to the church in the royal town, the coach suddenly stopped. The coachman got down and stepped over to an opening covered with a grating and spat into it.

"Why did you do that?" asked those inside the coach.

"It is the king's command. In the dungeon below that grating, they keep the former queen, who instead of children gave birth to puppies and kittens. That is why everyone who passes by must spit on her, or they will be severely punished."

"We won't do that," said the eldest brother.

"Why not?"

"Because that woman is a mother without children and we are children without a mother."

They refused to spit through the grating.

At this, the coach guards stepped up and led all three of them off to prison.

The king was sitting in his chamber, impatiently awaiting his young guests, when the guard came to report that those two young men and their sister had disobeyed the royal command, had refused to spit through the grating and had been thrown into prison.

"Well, let them stay there!" the king shouted in anger. "We can't have people disobeying royal commands whenever they happen to feel like it!"

He fumed and fretted and fussed and wrought his anger on anyone who happened to cross his path. But gradually his anger wore off and he began to feel sorry. He felt so very, very sorry — why should that be? When he just didn't know what to do with himself, he remembered once more that beautiful garden and in it the three magic things, which he had hardly noticed. He kept thinking about the bird who knew and revealed all, but of whom he had asked nothing.

The king once more drove off to visit that garden and asked to be led straight to that magic tree, where, on the lowest branch, the golden cage hung.

"Tell me, little bird, who knows everything, why I have no peace of mind, why my heart aches so?"

The bird began to sing as if playing on a silver string:

> *Your heart aches, Your Highness, for the injustice you*
> *have done to your near and your dear, to innocent lives.*
> *That is the secret, the bane of your life,*
> *unhappy man.*
> *Your wife gave birth to three beautiful children,*
> *two handsome sons, one pretty daughter,*
> *but her jealous sisters stole the children from her,*
> *sent them floating away at the mercy of the river.*
> *A good man saved your sons and your daughter,*
> *brought them up among the beauties of this, his garden,*
> *taught them to be good, hard-working and kind.*
> *When these children went to visit you, their true father,*
> *you, Your Royal Highness,*
> *they refused to spit on the queen, the mother they had*

never known,
and were thrown into prison at their father's command.
These are the reasons why your heart aches so...

As the bird sang, the king's eyes filled with tears. Then he asked the gardener whether those two young men and the girl were his own children.

The gardener told him that he could not love his own children more, but that, unfortunately, he was not their father. To his great happiness and joy, the river had brought them to him: first the boys and then the girl. It had been just about the time when their country had been attacked by its neighbours and a war had been waged on their borders.

The king embraced the gardener as if he were his brother, filled a jug of water that revives all and quickly returned to the royal town.

When they came to the grating beside the church, he ordered his servants to stop and open the dungeon. He went inside and fell on his knees in front of his tortured wife, who no longer had the strength to stand or sit, but just lay weak and helpless on the stones, a thousand times spat on from head to foot. The king took the jug with the water of life and gently wiped the queen's forehead. At this, the years of suffering miraculously fell away and she stood before him as young and as beautiful as she once had been. Hand in hand, they went out of the dungeon and asked to be led to their children in prison. Their joy cannot be put into words. The children flung their arms around their mother, around their father, they gazed into each other's eyes, unable to gaze their fill, listened to one another, unable to hear their fill. When they had recovered from their first flight of happiness, they quietly drove off to the palace together.

That very day, the king called a royal council, to which he invited the wives of the cook and chamberlain as well.

"We should like to hear your opinion," said the king. "Now tell us, what punishment is deserved by someone who sends innocent people to their deaths?"

The councillors advised one thing and another. In the end, the cook's wife spoke up, "I should send such a person to the same fate as he sent his victims."

118

"You have passed your own sentence," said the king, "on yourself and on your sister. You threw my children to the mercy of the waves and brought shame on my wife. The same shall happen to you."

They nailed the two sisters up into a big box and threw it into the river. The river spouted and spewed, the waves did not want to carry the box, they thrust it away from one to another, pushing it downstream to the open sea. Back and forth, back and forth it tossed on the waves. Back and forth, back and forth it tosses to this very day.

The king, the queen and their three children lived happily ever after. They richly rewarded the gardener, and when he grew old and could work no more, they took him to their palace to spend the rest of his life with them.

At the king's command, the three magic things were brought to the palace. The tree that adorns all grows in the middle of the garden. The water that revives all bubbles, sparkles and sprays up into the air. The bird that reveals all lives in its golden cage on the lowest branch and whenever anyone asks it anything, it tells them all it knows.

The Toad

Through a deep valley, there once flowed a mountain stream, but the stream dried up and the middle of the green meadow dried up too. All that remained growing there were four beech trees.

On that meadow, its back to the forest, there stood a wooden cottage, small and ramshackle, such as those that belong only to very poor people. In this cottage, there lived a mother with her son, Andrew. Andrew was a well-grown, strong young man and the farmers from the village liked to hire him for work. But it happened, as it often does, that Andrew fell in love with a rich farmer's daughter and she fell in love with him. At first, they just cast shy looks at each other, but it was not long before they spoke out and so Andrew plucked up courage to ask her father for her hand. The rich farmer soon sent him packing, "A miserable beggar like you, without a penny to your name and you have the impudence to ask me..."

Andrew went home feeling crushed and humiliated, tortured by sorrow and shame. He begged his mother to bake him a loaf of bread, sharpened his scythe and set out into the world.

He walked on and on until he came to the seventh, or perhaps, it was even the seventeenth village. There he hired himself out as a mower. As he mowed the huge meadow with the other men, who were strangers to him, he gradually forgot his sorrow. They had almost finished mowing the meadow when one of the men caught sight of a frog in the grass.

"Look at that bigbellied toad!" he called out.

"Ugh, what an ugly creature!" another spat.

"Step aside, I'll kill it with my scythe!" said a third.

The toad stared at him, its eyes bulging, it sensed that death was very near.

120

But Andrew said, "Leave it alone, even a toad is one of God's creatures!"

"Well, then, you put the beautiful creature in your pocket!" the first man scoffed at him and the others laughed in ridicule.

Taking no notice of their sneers, Andrew put the toad in his hat, gave it a piece of cheese and carried it to the edge of the meadow, far from human eyes.

The next day the mowers received their pay and each went his own way. Some went home and some went to look for further work.

Andrew also set off in search of something else. He kept going on and on, but it seemed he had chosen the wrong path, the countryside for far around was dry and deserted. A whole three days passed and he met not a living soul, or a hut, not even a cottage in sight. The food in his bundle was spent, he was dying of hunger and his thirst was even worse. It was getting dark, it would soon be night. Then, suddenly, a delicious smell met his nostrils! Not of lilies or roses, but of something that for him, at that moment, could not be more pleasant — the smell of roast pork and cabbage.

He followed his nose until he came to the lighted window of a house of some kind. The doors opened for him as he approached and his ears were filled with the noise of men talking and laughing... Why, it must be an inn!

"Welcome, Andrew!" the pretty innkeeper said. "I expected you to arrive yesterday." She led him to a table that was already laid, placed before him a plate of roast pork and cabbage and a bottle of good wine.

"How do you know my name?" asked Andrew, when he had satisfied his hunger and quenched his thirst.

"Don't ask that," she said. "The only thing I'll tell you is that it's a long time since I ate such good cheese as your."

Shivers ran down Andrew's spine, he remembered who he had given his cheese to, not long ago: the toad! For heavens' sake, what kind of an inn was this? All the guests were

dressed in the green clothes of foresters, their skins were dark as if tanned by the sun. They were drinking wine, playing cards, and their eyes were shining. Only one of them sat by himself in a corner, singing noisily. Clearly he had emptied too many cups. From time to time, the doors opened, more foresters came in, their stamping made a din like horses' hooves, but not one of them uttered a greeting, not one took his hat off.

"I'd better get out of here as soon as possible," Andrew thought to himself. But it was dark as pitch outside. He would have to wait until it began to get light, or he could break his neck in some ditch. He put his elbows on the table and his head on his elbows, as if overcome by sleep, but he was wide awake, his ears pricked up like those of a rabbit. The man in the corner soon began his rowdy song once more. If anyone listened carefully, he could make out these words from his drunken babble:

> *Through a deep valley*
> *Ran a mountain stream,*
> *Now dry is the meadow*
> *That once was so green.*
> *Dry is the meadow*
> *The grass is no more,*
> *But four tall beeches*
> *Stand there as of yore.*

Andrew very nearly jumped to his feet, the song seemed so familiar to him. Not that he had ever heard it before, but the place it described he knew only too well. Why, it must be the meadow where his own cottage stood. He forced himself to pretend that he was still asleep, and to make it more convincing, began to snore lightly. The one in the corner bleated on oblivious:

> *In the leaves of those trees*
> *The birds chirp and sing*
> *And under their roots*
> *Gold fit for a king.*
> *Under their roots,*
> *In a hole in the earth,*
> *A pile of gold ducats,*
> *A fortune they're worth.*

122

Andrew held his breath. Who knows what these guests would do if they knew he had heard their song. But they took no notice of him and in time they began to get up from the tables and noisily leave the inn. When Andrew dared lift his head at last, he saw that the inn was empty. The last guest was just passing the window, his hat had slipped to one side and sticking out from underneath it, was the horn of an old ram.

"You behaved well, Andrew," the innkeeper told him. "Just as you ought to. Make good use of what you heard. It is my reward for saving my life."

She refused to take any payment for the hospitality he had received, but accompanied him to the door and showed him the way home.

Before dusk fell, Andrew arrived home and that very night, he dug the treasure up from under the beech trees: two large chests full of gold ducats. No sooner had he carried them into the cottage with the help of his mother, than with a gushing and a rushing, water filled the dry bed of the stream, fish darted about and flowers burst into blossom on its banks.

The very first thing that Andrew did was to buy the meadow, together with the beech trees and the stream. There he built a house. He bought fields and cattle so he would be a real farmer. But he still had a lot of gold ducats to spare. One Sunday, he called all the children from the village to come to the meadow and he gave each and every one a gold ducat. That was the very first time that those who had a lot of children were glad they had so many and that those who had few were sorry they had so few.

That evening a rich farmer came to see Andrew. The very same one that had chased him out of his house before.

"Dear boy," he said to him, "you shouldn't do what you are doing. You are giving away your wealth to other people's children and forgetting about your own. After all, you wanted to get married. You asked for our Annie's hand. Well, if you are still of the same mind, I have nothing against you becoming one of our family."

Andrew was glad to hear this, because he really did love Anna. It was not long before the wedding took place. They invited guests from every house and I was among them. They had a wineskin at the wedding and all of a sudden it burst open, the wine rushed out and carried me off to my home.

The Werewolf

It happened somewhere far away, or maybe it was not so far as it was long ago, but if long ago, then far away, too.

In a word, there once lived a woman, Sybyl was her name, and she was very wise. She knew all kinds of things! She knew how to heal open wounds and closed wounds. She knew of a herb which opened the hiding places of treasure. She even knew of a herb which, when you put it in your right boot and kicked someone with it, they melted into a black puddle. Sybyl knew many secrets, but she was never satisfied. That is how it is in this world; he who has much, wants more, and he who knows much, wants to know even more.

In a book of witchcraft Sybyl happened to read about a herb that gives one the power to change anyone into anything. That herb flowered only once in seven years, its flower had to be plucked on a midsummer night, exactly at midnight, placed on the tongue and swallowed. Sybyl calculated that it was just then the seventh year, when the plant should flower and set out, taking an unknown path, as her book of witchcraft instructed. In the middle of a thick forest she found a meadow covered with thousands of flowers and with the help of her book found that rare herb. It was as brightly coloured as the wings of a butterfly. She sat down beside it and waited. When the stars showed it was midnight, she plucked the flower, placed it on her tongue and swallowed it. She did not notice that a red-poppy seed had stuck to it and she swallowed it together with the many-coloured flower. To swallow a red-poppy seed on such a night is extremely unlucky, and there is nothing even such a wise woman as Sybyl can do about it.

Not long after that, Sybyl discovered she was going to have a child and when it was born, it was a boy. But no ordinary boy! He immediately stood up on his legs, his ears were pointed and alert, his mouth full of teeth. He grew into an ill-natured boy, with an insatiable appetite. When he wasn't eating, he was sure to be prowling around the forest. Every few minutes, Sybyl would go to the magic window in the corner of her room, breathe on the glass and at once she saw where the boy was and what he was doing.

One day she looked through the window and caught sight of her son in a ravine a long way off. He was gnawing at something. She took a closer look and froze with horror. The boy was gnawing wolf-root! Her worst fears were confirmed — her son was a werewolf. She began to brew all kinds of magic herbs for him. These may well have changed his wolfish nature, if only he had drunk them. But he would secretly pour them away and more and more often he would go to the ravine and dig up wolf-root. Whenever he returned from there, he bared his teeth in a threatening manner and there was an evil glare in his eyes. Sybyl was very unhappy because of him and from then on, she thought of him as the werewolf, although he had a proper human name, Matthew.

One day a traveller from three villages away came to see Sybyl and she was not at home. The werewolf, who had just returned from the ravine, dragged the poor man immediately into the cottage and gobbled him up.

Sybyl returned home and her eye fell on a knapsack behind the front door.

"Who is here?" she asked.

"Why should there be anyone here?" the werewolf growled back.

"And what about the knapsack on the bench?"

"Oh, the knapsack! I found it. I found it in the ravine, it was lying beside a tree stump. Someone must have left it there. I thought you could use it for herbs and roots."

"What a lot he has to say all at once!" Sybyl stared at him in surprise. "At other times I can hardly get a word out of him."

"That's it, my son, people come here for advice and help," she said aloud.

"Let them come, they don't bother me!" the werewolf snarled back, his voice catching in his throat and making a sound like the howl of a wolf.

"I mustn't take my eyes off him" thought Sybyl. "While I am around, he won't dare to harm people."

But how could she keep her eyes on him all the time? One day she would be called to look at a sick woman, another she had to gather herbs or wash her clothes in the river. When she returned home she often found a walking stick, a basket, a pair of shoes or boots. Things that hadn't been there before. When she asked the werewolf who they belonged to, he didn't even try to explain, just laughed until he howled. His gaze got gradually fiercer, his eyes glared brightly and his nostrils widened. Sybyl did not need to be very wise to realize that something terrible was going on.

So Sybyl did not leave the cottage and if anyone came to see her she gave them what they needed and sent them away as soon as she could, often not even inviting them into the parlour, so that the werewolf would not see them.

One day the werewolf once more went off to the ravine and his mother saw him through her magic window, feeding on wolf-root. Just then an orphan girl came to see her. She had been sawing wood at a farm where she worked as a servant and the saw had slipped and cut her hand. The wound kept festering, it just would not heal. Sybyl led the girl into the house and was putting healing herbs on the wound, when she heard the werewolf calling from the yard, "Mother, who's in the house?"

"Why should there be anyone, Matthew?" Sybyl quickly slipped out of the house and secretly locked the door behind her, because the werewolf's voice seemed even more threatening than usual.

"Out with it, mother! I was in the ravine and I could see the yard from there. There were two of you!"

"Well, yes, there was a girl here with a wounded hand, but she left a long time ago."

"No, she didn't! You wouldn't have locked the door if she had. Get out of my way, mother."

"No, I won't my son."

The werewolf thrust his mother aside and wanted to break down the door, but it was a strong, oak door. So he ran off to the shed to fetch an iron bar. Sybyl lost no time, she quickly hurried inside, not even stopping to shut the door behind her. She placed her palm on the girl's head and changed her into a needle. She threaded the needle, sat down next to the window and began to mend her apron. The werewolf appeared in the doorway.

"You can see for yourself that no one is here!" said his mother.

"There must have been someone here just now, I can smell human flesh! You didn't want me to have her, mother, that's the last time, you hear?"

"I hear, my son," said Sybyl. She stuck the needle into the apron and rummaged through the herbs that were spread out all over the room. She found the one she was looking for and put it into her right boot. She put on her boots, as if she was getting ready to go to the village, stepped over to the werewolf and said.

"Today really was the last time, my son who, through no fault of your own, was born a werewolf." She kicked his ankle with her right boot, into which she had, a moment before, put the magic herb.

The werewolf howled in a terrible wolfish voice, fell to the ground and melted into a black puddle.

Sybyl then turned the needle back into a girl and said, "I didn't even have time to bandage your wound, my child, so show me it now. And if you want, well, you are an orphan and I am an orphan, you can stay with me if you like, we won't be lonely together."

The little girl stayed on to live in Sybyl's house and they grew very fond of each other. Sybyl taught her all kinds of things about her art, but not everything, not everything by far. She knew that not everyone can bear the burden of knowledge and that the price paid for it could at times be extremely cruel.

Mallica

It happened a long time ago, when words had a terrible, invincible power. When a word was uttered, it had to happen. Words of blessing could protect men from misfortune, or even save them from the jaws of death and the words of a curse could move heaven and earth.

In those times long ago there lived a king. His wife died and he decided to marry again, because he had long been attracted to a young princess from a neighboring kingdom. He was so much in love that he thought it wise not to mention his children when he asked for her hand in marriage. What will be, will be, he thought.

There was a splendid, grandiose wedding, they were still feasting and dancing and making merry on the seventh day. On that day, the young queen slipped away from the guests to have a look at the palace in which she was to live. She reached a remote wing of the building and opened the door to the terrace. There her gaze fell on seven boys of all ages playing together.

"Whose children are you?" asked the queen.

"We are the sons of the king of this country," said the oldest boy. "And who are you?"

"I am... I..."

The young queen stared dumbfounded at the king's sons, her step-sons, and her heart filled with hate. Words as dangerous as snake's poison sprang to her lips. She could not hold them back and spat them out, "May you turn into... into ducks!"

She had hardly uttered these words and the seven princes changed into seven gold-crested white ducks, which flapped their wings and, quacking terribly, rose up into the air. A moment later there was not a trace of them left and the queen rejoined her wedding guests as if nothing had happened. She had not noticed that someone was standing behind a pillar on the terrace, someone who had seen and heard everything. It was Princess Barbara, who had been keeping an eye on her youngest brother while their nurse had been washing the dishes for the wedding feast.

Barbara wept bitter tears for her brothers and resolved that she would go out into the world, then and there, and not return until she had found her brothers and freed them. She wrapped a few things up in a bundle and left the palace. No one saw how, when or which way she went.

She travelled not one day, not two, but many, many days until, at last, she came to a desert place where there grew neither trees, nor bushes, not even grass. It was evening when she arrived at a little house. It was the house of Little Star. She was just cleaning her lamp before lighting it.

"Good evening to you, Little Star," Barbara greeted her.

"Good evening to you, too, little girl. Where have you come from? This is so far from anywhere, you can never hear a dog bark or a cock crow."

"I am looking for my seven brothers, seven white ducks with golden crests. Have you seen them, Little Star?"

"I haven't seen them, little girl, but if you like, I'll take you to my brother, Little Moon. Maybe he will know something."

They went to see Little Moon, but they didn't find him at home, he had already gone to work for the night.

"Don't worry," said Little Star, "we'll go and ask my other brother, Little Sun."

Little Sun was already lying in his golden bed, but he was not yet asleep, he was telling his mother all he had seen that day. Just then Little Star and Barbara arrived.

"Good evening, mother, good evening, brother Sun." Little Star greeted them. "This girl is Barbara and she is looking for her seven brothers, seven white ducks with golden crests. Have you seen them, brother?"

"Wait a minute... seven ducks, you say, with golden crests... Of

130

course I have! I have been watching them for some time on a green meadow in Egypt. They graze there and cannot fly away. That is the curse that has been put on them. You are sure to find them there Barbara."

"What were your brothers like when they were still at home," asked Little Sun's mother.

"What were they like?" mused Barbara. "Well, like all boys, I suppose. The first brother loved hunting, the second liked fencing, the third loved dancing, the fourth only ate, the fifth adored almond sauce, the sixth his rocking horse, and the seventh, still a baby, was fondest of sucking his thumb."

"A rocking horse . . . his thumb, quite the same as my children when they were little," Mother Sun said whistfully. "So they are in Egypt! But that is terribly far away, you even have to cross the sea!" She turned to Little Sun, "Couldn't we lend Barbara those magic slippers of ours which, when anyone puts them on, take them wherever they like?"

Barbara borrowed the magic slippers, put them on and wished, "Take me at once to that green meadow in Egypt where my brothers are grazing."

No sooner had she said that, than she was there.

The seven white ducks lifted their gold-crested heads and recognized their sister immediately. They greeted her with quacks of joy, "Welcome, Barbara, how did you find us?"

She told them everything and then asked, "Tell me, my white brothers, how can I set you free?"

"We'll tell you all we know," said the eldest duck. "And all we know is mallica."

"Mallica, that is all we know," said the other six ducks sadly.

"And what is mallica? A witch? Or a magic stone of some kind? Or snake's fat? Or what?"

The white ducks just shook their heads sadly to show that they really did not know.

Barbara thought hard, racking her brains who she should ask. In the end, she had an idea, she put on the magic slippers and in a flash she was not in the green meadow in Egypt, but standing in front of the shelves of the royal library in her father's palace. There were a lot of books there, maybe a thousand or even one thousand five hundred, in those days that was a very large number, and apart from Barbara there was not a living soul there. Barbara pulled out a book as big as a quarter of the table, looked through it carefully, but could not find a single mention of mallica. She pulled out a bigger book that covered half the table, she looked and looked, but still not a word about mallica. Finally, she pulled out an enormous book as big as the table itself, looked and looked, but there was not a word, not even half, not even a quarter of a word about it. Barbara was very disappointed and once more began to rack her brains who she could consult. It occurred to her that of all the people she knew the wisest was their old nurse, who had brought them up and taken care of them as if she had been their mother. So she put on the slippers and was there in a flash.

Ever since the royal children had disappeared, the nurse had looked for them day after day, asking everyone she met if they had seen them. She had just come home from this daily search, when she suddenly found Barbara in front of her. She was sitting in her little room, smiling sweetly as if nothing had happened, as if the seven brothers had not disappeared. They were both delighted to see each

other, they hugged each other and talked and talked. When they had told all, Barbara suddenly said, "Old people are usually wise, they sometimes even know things which are not to be found in books. Do you know, by any chance, who or what is mallica?"

"Mallica, mallica, it does ring a bell...

Ah, wait a minute! When I was still a little girl, like you are now, we had a black pig with a long nose and my mother always used to say of it: 'That pig is a real gourmet. He'd do anything for mallica.' But what it was, I really can't tell you.''

"Thank you, dear nurse, that may help," said Barbara. She put on

the slippers and wished, "Take me to where my nurse lived when she was little.''

In a moment, she was there.

A leafy forest, at the edge of the forest a white cottage and a little way off a boy grazing pigs.

"Good day," Barbara greeted him. "Do you know what mallica is?''

The boy shook his head.

"Then tell me at least, which of these pigs is fondest of eating?''

"They are all fond of eating," the boy said, "but the one who really enjoys it most, is that black one with the long nose. He takes no notice of acorns, but he keeps digging up roots of some sort.''

"Maybe he inherited the habit from his great-grandmother," thought Barbara and her heart beat excitedly.

"Could you give me one of those roots?''

"Of course, just wait a minute. Ah, it's just dug one up!" the boy ran over to the pig to snatch the root away, but hum! It swallowed it whole.

"Greedy beast! You see, I must be quicker!''

After a while the pig dug up another root. The boy stole up behind it and rapped it on its snout with a stick. The pig squealed and let go of the root.

"Here you are, pretty girl," the boy gave it to Barbara. "And now tell me, what do you want it for?"

"You know, maybe this white root is the mallica I'm looking for. If so, it will save my seven brothers."

She thanked him for his help, put on her magic slippers and thought, "Take me back to the green meadow in Egypt where my brothers are grazing."

Suddenly, she was there.

With hands shaking, she divided the white root into seven pieces and gave them to the ducks. The first duck ate his piece, and nothing, absolutely nothing happened. The second ate his piece, too, and once again, nothing. The third, fourth, fifth and sixth swallowed theirs and nothing, nothing, nothing happened at all. Only the seventh, the

youngest duckling, was still struggling with his piece, he couldn't swallow it. Eventually he did manage to get it down and then... The whole flock flapped its wings and at that very moment instead of ducks, there were seven handsome boys in the meadow. The very same as those of whom the first loved hunting, the second liked fencing, the third loved dancing, the fourth only eating, the fifth adored almond sauce, the sixth his rocking horse, and the seventh, still a baby, was fondest of sucking his thumb.

The brothers threw their arms around their faithful sister and she hugged them. Then they set off for the sea, where they found a ship that was sailing to their country. They begged the sailors to take them across the sea and soon they set sail for home.

Who knows how, but the rumour that the seven princes and Princess Barbara were returning to their father flew across the sea like the wind and reached the royal town. The king immediately had twelve fiery stallions shod with silver horseshoes so that they would ring out on the stones and send sparks flying all the way. With his three most beautiful coaches, the king went to meet his children at the seashore. The people rejoiced with their king and sung the praises of him and his beautiful children. On the way Barbara did not forget to return the magic slippers, without which it would hardly have been possible to save her brothers.

The king was very happy to see his children, but he was also at a loss to know what to do with his young wife. Finally it occurred to him to ask her what she would do with someone who tried to destroy seven innocent lives. Whatever she said, she would have.

But the queen had no wish to meet her step-children. She knew that nothing good awaited her in that country and she preferred to return to the land from where she had come.

The Witches

Once upon a time, who knows when, but one time or other, there lived near a lake, at the foot of the mountains, a horde of witches, really ugly hags. They did not wash, they did not comb their hair, they could hardly be bothered even to bring up their own children. But how they loved to eat! Their favorite titbit was juicy red carrots, which they stole from the peasants' gardens at night.

One night they were stealing carrots in a garden belonging to young Sigrid and her husband, Sigmund. The witches ate their fill and then peeped in through the window as they were curious to know why there was a light in the room. Sigrid had given birth only a week before and she was nursing her beautiful baby. She finished feeding her little son and was putting him in his wooden cradle, when she suddenly heard a knocking on the window: clop, clop, clop!

"Who's there?" Sigrid peered out of the window.

She could not see anyone, but she could hear the heartrending crying of a child around the corner of the house. She felt sorry for the child and her first thought was to wake up her husband. However, she could not bring herself to disturb his dream, he had been so tired after a hard day, and so she went out of the house by herself. She had hardly put a foot outside when the witches caught hold of her and whirled her off to their lake. Once there, the ugly hags all crowded around her, jumping up and down, with cries of "Welcome, Sigrid! Now you will live with us, nurse our children and wash their nappies."

There were hordes of children there, all of them hungry, and dirty.

It was terrible for Sigrid to have to nurse these ugly witch-children instead of her own little son and she tried to run away. But the witches caught her and dragged her back to the lake by her hair. She did not try it again, because her strength ebbed fast, she grew so thin and weak she could hardly stand on her feet.

Thus a year passed.

Once Sigrid was washing nappies on the banks of the stream that flowed into the lake, when she heard the sound of human footsteps. Who dared to come so near to the lake? It was a man from the village, who was looking for a stray sheep.

"Hey there, good neighbor!" called Sigrid.

He stopped and stared, not recognizing her at all.

"Why do you call me neighbor, when I have never seen you in my life before?!"

"Take a better look at me! I am Sigrid! For a year now I have had to nurse the witches' children, they have sucked all the blood from me, taken all my strength away, that's why you can't recognize me."

"And we all thought you were dead," said the neighbor. "How your husband grieved for you, and your father and mother! What message should I give them from you?"

"Tell them that if they do what I tell them, they can set me free. But remember exactly what I say: tomorrow morning, my husband Sigmund must buy up all the carrots in the whole village, so that there isn't a carrot left in the fields or gardens. He must put all these carrots on a wagon and harness his best horses to it. Then he must come here a week from now. I shall be waiting for him at this spot.

Quite forgetting about his stray sheep, the neighbor hurried off home to pass on the message as quickly as possible.

Sigmund did exactly as he was instructed and a week later, he arrived at the stream with the wagon. Sigrid was waiting for him there. She quickly climbed up into the wagon and they drove off as fast as they could go.

But the witches discovered in no time that Sigrid had run away again, and a whole flock of them flew after her. When they were just about to catch up with the wagon, Sigrid threw them an armful of carrots. The witches pounced on the carrots, fighting over them, tearing each other's hair, screaming and screeching. They were so hungry for carrots after a week's fasting. It was quite a while before they noticed that the wagon was a long way off and they hurried after it. But Sigrid threw them another armful of carrots, and while the witches squabbled and fought over it, the wagon gained ground on them. In this way, Sigrid gradually threw them all the carrots, and just as she was throwing the last armful the horses reached the edge of the village.

So Sigrid was saved and in time, with the help of her good husband and dear little son, she grew stronger and her beauty returned.

But from that time on all the women who were nursing babies did not dare to venture out into the yard, they were so afraid the witches would drag them away to nurse their children. The whole village lived in continuous fear. More afraid than anyone else was Sigrid. Not only at night, but during the day, too, she did not so much as dare to go out of the room and she kept her child shut between four walls as well.

Sigmund did not like this at all. He began to rack his brains how he could help his wife. Then an idea struck him.

When spring came, he sowed in the garden twice as many carrots as in other years and they came up beautiful, big and juicy. On moonlit nights he watched the witches when they came to steal them, their crunching and munching could be heard even from inside the house. One day he carried out to the vegetable patch one of his wife's boots, not just any old one, but one of her best Sunday boots, which she had worn at their wedding. That night the witches appeared again in search of the carrots and while they were eating their fill, one of them found the boot.

"Ah, look what I've found!" she called out joyfully, because the boot shone beautifully in the light of the moon.

"Give it to me!" another snatched it from her.

"No, give it to me!"

"I want it!"

They snatched the boot from hand to hand, peering inside it.

In the end, the most experienced of them said, "That is what human women wear on their feet and it looks very pretty. It makes a nice clicking or sometimes crunching sound."

Hearing this, the witch who had just snatched the boot from another, stuck both feet into it at once. She tried to walk, because she wanted to hear that clicking or crunching noise, but instead of that, she fell flat on her nose in the middle of the vegetable patch. She tried

to get up, but she couldn't. The others danced round her, laughing and shrieking, so that they could be heard for far around.

At that moment, Sigmund stepped out into the yard, whirled his whip around his head and cracked it so loud that the dogs in the next village began barking. The witches took fright and flew off, they were back in their lake in no time. Only the one who was imprisoned in the boot remained lying on the vegetable patch, she couldn't even manage to hop away to the fence. Sigmund strode over to her, tied a chain around her waist, dragged her off into the hall and fastened her securely to the bench. The witch twisted and turned, sweeping the hall with her green hair, making the whole house reek of mire.

"Let me go, good man!" she wailed, "I'll never steal your carrots again!"

"I'll let you go," said Sigmund, "if you tell me when you witches will disappear from our lake."

"That lake isn't yours!" the witch spat back, "we've been living there longer than you have in this village. In that lake, under a red stone, there is a pearl like an ox's eye. I'll give it to you if you let me go."

"I'll let you go," repeated Sigmund, "when you tell me when you witches will disappear from our lake."

"That lake is ours!" the witch beat on the bench with her fist. "We were living there even when the king of the wind ruled this country. Once he flew over the lake on his magic stallion and his gold crown fell off his head. I'll bring you that crown, if you let me go."

"I'll only let you go," Sigmund repeated dauntlessly, "if you tell me when you witches will disappear from our lake."

"Why should I tell you when anyway it will never happen."

"What will never happen?"

"That someone will do what has to be done if we witches are to be forced to leave."

"And what is that?"

"Well, a man from your village would have to pass through a keyhole. And no one will ever manage that. So let me go, Sigmund! I'll bring you the golden fish that sleeps in a silver nook. That fish will fulfill three wishes: one for you, one for your wife and one for your son."

"And is that all?" asked Sigmund. "Just to pass through a keyhole, nothing more? You know, even if none of us ever manages to do it, I should like to know all the same."

"Very well, if you insist. Well, if someone did manage to pass through a keyhole, that man would still have to spit in the eyes of a witch and, facing three peaks in turn, say 'May you vanish for good!' Now you must let me go."

"I'll let you go, but I must first make sure you have told me the truth," said Sigmund.

He took himself off to the blacksmith's and said to him, "Listen, blacksmith, could you make me such a big lock that I could pass through the keyhole?"

"And what door do you want to fix it in?" laughed the blacksmith.

"This is no laughing matter," said Sigmund, "Don't waste time and get down to work, if you want your wife to be left in peace by the witches."

The blacksmith's wife was due to have a baby shortly, and so the craftsman set to work with his journeymen. It was a hard task, the sparks went flying all over the forge. Three days later, the lock was ready. What a lock it was! An enormous thing! Sigmund had to bring a wagon to fetch it and it was as much as twelve men could do to heave the keyhole on to it. They drove the wagon to Sigmund's yard, where they stood the keyhole up, supporting it on its own huge key. With the whole village watching, they remember it to this very day, Sigmund crawled through the keyhole, went into the hall, spat in the witch's eyes and facing three peaks in turn, declared, "May you vanish for good!" The witch cried out like a child, so that everyone looked around to see which child's foot had been stepped on. When they looked back at the bench in the hall, there was only an empty chain and a tangle of green hair.

From that time on no one saw the witches near that village. The carrots grew undisturbed in the vegetable patches, and what is most important, the women and little children no longer had to hide in fear, nothing happened to any of them again.

The men carried the huge lock to the village green and stood it up there, just in case they should ever need it again. The children, who grazed the geese, played around it, crawling through the keyhole and singing,

> *The golden gate is open,*
> *leaning on its golden key.*
> *If you crawl inside there,*
> *an apple you will see.*
> *Be you he or be you she,*
> *We'll not set you free.*

Over the years the lock and the key turned rusty and wasted away, until there was no trace of them left, just this tale and the game "golden gate" which children still like to play to this very day.

The Third Brother

There was once a footbridge over a muddy stream and in a cottage nearby, there lived a widow. Her husband had died a long time before, but happily she was not left alone in the world, for she had three children: two sons, already young men and a girl as pretty as a rose.

One day the sons said to their mother, "Tomorrow we shall be ploughing in a new field, far away at the foot of the mountain. Send our sister with our lunch."

"Of course I'll bring it," said their sister, "but how shall I find you if it's a new field a long way off?"

The brothers thought for a moment, scratching their heads, and then they said, "When we get to the edge of the village we'll begin to plough a furrow which will lead to the new field. Follow that furrow and you'll find us."

That is what they did. They ploughed up a furrow as far as the new field and worked there in peace.

Very well. So far, so good.

But on the other side of that mountain there lived a seven-headed dragon, Wild-eye, who had long had his eye on the widow's daughter. He used to stare at her from afar with his wild eyes and black thoughts came into his huge heads. When he caught sight of the furrow the brothers had ploughed, he was delighted. He galloped over to it on his horse, trampled it down and ploughed up another, which led straight to his castle.

Before noon the sister wrapped her brothers' lunch up in a bundle and set off along the furrow. She went on and on for a long, long time. "What a long way away they are," she thought, because it was already some hours after noon and there was no sign of her brothers. It had begun to grow dark and night was approaching when the girl

143

caught sight of a castle in front of her: its ramparts stood out against the clear sky like huge, black dragon's teeth.

Wildeye, the dragon, came running out of the castle. "Welcome, beautiful girl, I've been waiting for you for so long!" and he looked her up and down from all sides. "Do you know that close up, you are even more beautiful than from afar? From now on, you will live with me here and scratch my heads for me. I'm terribly fond of that. And you will look after me as a good wife should look after her husband."

The girl burst into tears and wrung her hands. But what could she do?

That evening the sons returned from their ploughing and reproached their mother for letting them go hungry the whole day.

"But your sister took you your lunch, you mean she didn't come?" their mother exclaimed anxiously.

"She didn't come."

They knew at once that something must have happened to her, but even so they waited a day or two to see whether she would return. They waited in vain. Then the elder son said, "Mother dear, I am going to look for our sister and I shall not return without her."

Very well. So far, so good.

As the young man was leaving the village he looked carefully at the furrow — why, it wasn't the one they had ploughed, it was quite a different one!

He set out to follow it. He went on and on until he came to a pasture, where an old man was grazing a herd of oxen.

"Good day to you, sir!"

"Good day to you, too, young man," replied the old herdsman. "You've chosen an ill way to go, take my advice and turn back. This furrow leads to the castle of Wildeye, the dragon."

"If that's so, then Wildeye, the dragon, has stolen my sister and I must go to free her."

"You are wasting your efforts, young man," said the herdsman, "no man is a match for the dragon. Just imagine, everyday he eats one ox from this herd, which I have to graze for him. Every day he drinks a spring full of magic water. Do you think you could eat a whole ox at one sitting? Just try!"

"It's not worth trying, one leg would be more than enough for me for three days."

"Then take the advice of an old man and go home at once. Isn't it bad enough that you have lost your sister?"

But the young man would not let himself be persuaded. After all, he had promised his mother that he would not return without his sister.

He went on his way until he came to a second pasture, where an old herdsman was grazing a herd of horses.

"A good day to you, sir."

"A good day to you, too, young man. You have chosen an ill-fated path to follow, this furrow leads to the castle of Wildeye, the dragon."

"I know that, sir. Wildeye, the dragon has stolen my sister, so I am going to free her."

"Well, jump up on one of these horses and try to gallop around this pasture three times before this piece of tow burns out."

The young man leapt up on a horse and the old man lighted the tow. The tow flared up and the horse raced on, but it had not got around even half the pasture before the tow burnt out.

"Well, young man, don't you go provoking the dragon, or not only will you fail to free your sister, but you'll leave your own bones there too. Isn't one lost life enough?" said the old man.

But the young man would not let himself be persuaded. After all, he had promised his mother not to return without his sister.

So he went on along that furrow until at last the castle came into view. It's ramparts stood out against the clear sky like huge, black dragon's teeth, and he knew at once that this was the castle of Wildeye, the dragon.

The young lad banged on the gate and it clanged and boomed back at him because it was made of iron. A window in the castle opened and his sister looked out, her face was sad and tear-stained.

"Who's there?" she asked.

"Open the gates, sister, it's me, your brother!"

"Oh, brother dear, quickly turn around and run off home, my husband will be back any moment and he is a seven-headed dragon."

"You must open the gates, sister, maybe I can come to some agreement with my brother-in-law. Are you going to leave me standing here outside?"

So his sister opened the gates and let him in. They hadn't even time to exchange a few words before a loud thud was heard in the courtyard.

"Oh, the dragon is coming home," said his sister, turning pale. "He throws his five-ton club ahead of him, so that he doesn't have to carry it."

A moment later the doors flung open and the dragon appeared.

"Welcome, brother-in-law! It's nice of you to come and visit me," he roared, looking the young man up and down derisively. "What a skinny little thing you are, dear brother-in-law, no doubt they don't give you enough to eat. Well, come on, I'll show you what gives a man strength!"

He opened the door to the next room and there a table with a whole roast ox awaited them.

"Sit down and eat!"

The dragon tore the roast ox apart and began to gobble it up. Before the young lad had time to realize what was happening, the meat had disappeared, not even a tiny little bone was left.

"Well, and now we've eaten, we'll go and race each other. Choose a horse from the stable, we'll gallop to the third valley from here and back."

The dragon leapt up on his horse and was gone in a cloud of dust. The young man had hardly managed to get a short way from the castle when the dragon returned, invigorated, as if he had drawn new strength from somewhere.

"You're good for nothing, brother-in-law! You bring shame on a self-respecting dragon!" declared Wildeye and dealt the young man such a blow in the chest that he flew off his horse and fell lifeless to the ground. The dragon picked him up under his arm and threw him onto a shelf in his pantry.

His sister wept and wept, she almost died of sorrow. She washed her brother from head to foot with her tears, but all in vain, he did not regain consciousness. From that day on, she was even more unhappy.

At home, their mother waited and waited. She wore a dip in the ground before the door, she spent so much time standing there gazing around in the hope of seeing her children coming back home.

The younger son could no longer bear to watch his mother's suffering, and he, himself, could not live in peace at home while who knows what had happened to his brother out there in the world. So one day, he announced that he, too, was going to look for his sister and his brother.

Very well. So far, so good.

He set out along the furrow the dragon had ploughed and exactly the same happened to him as to his elder brother. The dragon sat him down before the roast ox, but quickly gobbled it all up by himself and then made him race him to the third valley. By the time the young man had chosen his horse and set off at a gallop, the dragon arrived home. With a roar of laughter, he dealt the young lad a blow in the chest that sent him falling lifeless to the ground. Then he carried him off under his arm and threw him on the shelf in the pantry where his elder brother lay.

Weeks passed and the weeks changed into months and the months into years. Their poor mother waited and waited, never giving up hope, even though she knew that her children must have met with some terrible misfortune. She lived alone in her cottage, sorrow and loneliness eating more and more into her heart. "If only I had someone to talk to," she sighed many a time.

One day she went to cut grass for her cow and as she was mowing, a little man hardly a hand high jumped up from under her sickle.

"Oh, my goodness, I very nearly cut you in half! What are you doing playing around in the grass!" she exclaimed, seemingly angry, but a smile came over her face. "What a lovely little fellow you are. Who are you?"

"I can be yours, if you want," said the little man and smiled back at her.

"Oh, I do want!" the woman cried out in joy. "Of course, I do. I have lost three children, so you can be my fourth."

"Very well, mother. Call me Leon and bring me up on mare's milk, that will make me as strong as a lion. When I get my strength up, I'll go out into the world and I'll bring back your three children."

"What can you do, you little thing, you can hardly be seen in the grass!" the woman smiled. She put Leon into her apron, heaved the bundle of grass up on her back and set off for home. Nevertheless, she did as he wanted and fed him a whole year on mare's milk. Leon grew strong and powerful even though he was still small. He had to be careful how he used his strength because when he dealt a blow, he could break a table or knock down a wall.

When a year had passed, he said to his mother, "Now feed me with meat, that will make me twice as strong, and then I shall go to look for my brothers and sister."

But his mother tried to dissuade him.

"Stop thinking about that, Leon, or you'll come to a sorry end, too. What would I do all alone in this hard world?"

"Don't you worry, mother, just you prepare that meat for me to temper my strength."

His mother had nothing else, only her cow, so she had it killed and roasted and stewed meat for her son, Leon. Wonder of wonders, she could not stew and roast the meat as fast as Leon could eat it. By the time evening came, all that remained of the cow was the bones.

"Now, mother dear, I'm as I should be and I can set out into the world."

Very well. So far, so good.

He strode along, following the furrow as his brothers had several years earlier, until he came to the pasture where the old herdsman was grazing the herd of oxen.

"A good day to you, sir!" Leon greeted him. "Tell me, please, have you seen two young men who were looking for their sister?"

"Yes, indeed, young man, I did see them! I saw them go in that

direction, but I didn't see them return. That's no wonder, the furrow they were following, like you, leads to the castle of Wildeye, the dragon. You just turn around and go back from where you have come. Don't hurry to your death."

"Don't try to dissuade me, sir, but rather advise me what to do to get the better of the dragon and free my brothers and sister."

"What can I tell you, young lad? Every evening the dragon must drink a springful of magic water, or it would lose its strength, but before that he always eats a roast ox, from this very herd which I am grazing. I would be glad to have done with this shameful work, I'd be only too glad to meet a man who could overcome the dragon. But that man must also be capable of eating a whole ox at once. And you... why, you don't even reach up to my knee."

Hearing these words, Leon laughed out loud, jumped up on the back of one of the oxen, dealt it a heavy blow over the head with his fist and it rolled over with its hoofs in the air. Then Leon made a fire and roasted the ox. Before you could count to ten, there was nothing left of the ox except a little piece the old herdsman managed to hide for his supper.

"Well, you are a real man and so far as eating goes, you are certainly a match for Wildeye," said the old man. "Good luck, then."

Leon went on his way and soon came to the second pasture, where the old herdsman was grazing the herd of horses.

"A good day to you, sir," Leon greeted him.

"A good day to you, young lad," the herdsman replied.

"You haven't, by any chance, seen two young men who were looking for their sister some time ago? They were my brothers."

"Yes, indeed, they did go this way, first one, then the other. They took no heed of my warning. At least you must listen to me and return, because this road leads to the castle of Wildeye, the dragon."

"That is just where I want to go, sir, so don't try to change my mind. Tell me, rather, what I have to do to overcome the dragon."

"I should be only too glad if you succeeded, my son, at least I should be freed at last from this shameful work, grazing the dragon's horses. How many people this ugly monster has already sent to their deaths! Well, look, young lad, if you can gallop around this pasture

150

three times before a piece of tow burns out, then you are the man who can get the better of the dragon.''

The old man pulled out a piece of tow, lit it and the fibre flared up. Leon was already on his horse and galloping around the pasture like lightning. The horse sensed that the man sitting on him had been brought up on mare's milk and flew like a whirlwind. The tow was still burning strongly, when Leon galloped around the pasture for the third time and came to a halt in front of the old herdsman.

''You're a man, indeed, Leon. Not even Wildeye, the dragon, can fly so fast,'' the herdsman praised him. ''Keep that horse, you will find it useful, because every evening, after supper, the dragon gallops off to the third valley to drink magic water which springs up in everlasting flames. If just one single day it did not drink this water, it would lose all its strength. You must hurry and get there first, then you'll see what will happen.''

Leon thanked the old man very much and set out on the next stage of his journey. He recognized the dragon's castle from a long way off, because the ramparts stood out against the clear sky like huge, black dragon's teeth.

Leon banged on the gates. A pretty young woman looked out of the window and he immediately guessed that this was his sister.

''Who's there?'' she asked.

''I'm your brother, Leon.''

''I have no brothers any longer,'' said the young woman, tears springing to her eyes.

''Yes, you have, sister, you have me. Your mother found me in the grass when she was mowing, a long time after you three had left her.''

''Whether you are my brother or not, go home while you have the chance. Those who came to fetch me from this castle have lost their lives. It would have been better if I'd never been born!''

But Leon begged her to let him in and so, in the end, she opened the gates and led him inside. They had hardly sat down and exchanged a word or two, when a terrible thump was heard in the courtyard.

"That's my husband coming home," said the young woman, turning pale. "He throws his five-ton club ahead of him, so that he doesn't have to carry it."

Hearing this, Leon ran out into the courtyard, caught the club as if it were just a little stone and threw it back, sending it whistling through the air.

Some time later, Wildeye, the dragon, rushed through the door. Flames were darting from his jaws.

"Was it you who threw my club back at me?" he growled at Leon, engulfing him in flames.

"Yes, that was me, brother-in-law, so that you would know what kind of a man you'd have to deal with."

The dragon hesitated, "Very well, very well," he said, "we'll compare our strength, but first we'll eat." He opened the door to the next room, where a table with an ox awaited them. They sat down at the table and set to eating. But the dragon hadn't time to satisfy even the worst of his hunger before Leon had devoured the whole ox.

"You're a better man than you look," said the dragon hoarsely. "Wait for me here, while I take a drink from my spring."

"You don't want to leave your guest thirsty, do you?" laughed Leon. "You'll not get away with that!" He leapt up on his horse and flew off to the third valley. He was there before Wildeye, but where was the spring of magic water that sprung up in everlasting flames? Leon rode to and fro across the valley, straining his eyes like a hawk, but the sun was just going down over the mountain and it flooded the whole valley with its fiery light. Leon seized his hat and threw it at the sun. The hat fell across the burning face of the sun and darkness fell in the valley, as if clouds had covered the sky. In that instant, Leon caught sight of a little light, a little flame flickering beside a stone. He rolled the stone away and in the hollow, he saw burning water springing up in flames, red and yellow tongues of fire. Leon lay down beside the spring and drank all the burning water at one gulp, so that there was not a drop left. At once he felt such a great strength well up

inside him that he could have broken the valley in two with the wave of a hand.

At this point, the dragon came racing up and when he saw that the spring under the rock was already drunk dry, he let out a roar that almost tore the trees up by their roots. He charged at Leon, dealing him a blow in the chest that was intended to be fatal. But he had miscalculated. It was not Leon, but he, himself that fell, bouncing off Leon's chest like a clod of earth off a rock and falling flat on the ground.

"It's true you are stronger than I am," groaned the dragon, staggering to his feet. "Let me get to the spring, to drink at least a drop, or I shall die of thirst."

"Die, you scoundrel! You killed my brothers!"

"I'll bring your brothers back to life, just let me drink the burning water. I have an ointment... on the shelf in the pantry... Let me drink..."

Leon bent over the spring, where a few drops were bubbling up again with little flames sparkling in them. He lifted a rock, then a second and a third, and the burning spring disappeared in the depths, as if it had never existed.

"The earth gave it strength, let the earth take it back again, so that never more can any monster make it his own."

Wildeye, the dragon, let out a howl and beat his tail, but he was already so weak that he could not drag himself to his feet. As he rolled about on the ground, he began to sink deeper and deeper. When he had quite disappeared from sight, leaving not a trace behind him, Leon sat astride his horse and returned to the castle. He went straight to the pantry, where he found the magic ointment. He rubbed it on his brothers and they sprang to their feet, alive and well.

The brothers flung their arms around their sister and joyfully welcomed among them the brother they had not known until then. When they had got over their excitement, they took silver, gold and precious stones from the castle and set off home. On the way, they were joined by the old herdsman with his horses and the other herdsman with the herd of oxen. They were both extremely glad that they no longer had to serve the cruel dragon, Wildeye.

Very well. So far, so good.

Everything would have been as it should be, if the two brothers had not felt more and more ashamed of themselves in Leon's company. What would people think of them if this little dwarf had succeeded where they had failed, and even had saved their lives! A little midget that wasn't even born like a human, but whom their mother had found somewhere in the grass. Why, they would be ashamed to look people in the face!

"Listen," whispered the elder brother to the younger one. "What about getting rid of him?"

They begun to discuss what would be the easiest way of ridding themselves of him and they did not notice that Leon was sitting just on the other side of the bush, where he could hear everything they said. They agreed that when they got near the village, they would lure Leon onto the footbridge, from where — as if by some unlucky chance — he would fall into the river.

Leon felt hurt, but he said nothing. He turned on his heel and, saying goodbye to no one, waving to no one, he disappeared into the thick grass. No one ever saw him again.

When the others had returned home and their mother had pressed the three children to her heart, her eyes gazed around in search of the fourth. Where was Leon? How come that he had not returned with them? Had they harmed him in any way? Had they offended him? Her joy was not entire and her heart began to ache. It ached and ached, it never stopped, as if its strength was ebbing away. She always felt at her best when she went out into the meadow and sat down in the grass. At such times, it seemed to her that Leon, the beloved little son she had found there, was somewhere near at hand.

The Race of Women

Once upon a time, but a long, long time ago, there were far fewer women than men. As there were so few of them, the father who gave his daughter's hand in marriage did not have to give her a dowry, but quite the opposite, the husband-to-be had to give the father all kinds of gifts: a length of linen and two furs, four sheep and a barrel of mead. If the bride was beautiful, the suitor offered an ox as well. If she was a young girl, he had to give a cow and calf into the bargain.

It once happened in those times that a father promised his daughter to three suitors at once. The first made a suitable offer, so the father promised her to him. The second made a suitable offer, plus something extra. "Very well, you can come for her tomorrow." The third made a suitable offer, plus something extra and a sack of salt on top of that. "Come tomorrow, the bargain is sealed."

So it happened that the next day three husbands-to-be were seen approaching the cottage, each of them bringing sheep, rams, a length of cloth, a barrel and furs.

The father was in a tricky situation, what now?

He caught the girl by the hand and pushed her into the pigpen, where he kept his pig and goat.

"Sit here and don't budge until

I let you out myself!'' he warned her.

The suitors arrived and asked for their young bride.

"She's gone to visit her aunt in the next village," her father tried to give an excuse. "Come back another day."

But the young men were already boiling with rage and insult, it was clear to each of them that the girl's father was making fools of them. They began to poke about the cottage in search of the girl, they would share her between them somehow.

The father could hardly bear the suspense, he knew that no good would come of this. It would surely end up in a fight. If only they would not open the pigpen! But the young men were already there!

"That's the pigpen, where I keep my pig and my goat," said the father shaking from head to foot and he began to mutter something secret and unintelligible, as if he were evoking some supernatural powers... That is, in fact, what he did.

The husbands-to-be opened the pigpen and what should they see? Three crouching girls: the first and the second were like two peas, the second and third were like two peas and the third was the spitting image of the other two.

The young men laughed, "You sly old man, what a place to hide our brides!"

They quite forgot their anger, handed over their gifts to the father, prepared three weddings in one and then each of them led his wife off to his own cottage.

It seemed that all had turned out well, but from that time on the father had no peace of mind. He had received gifts for three girls, but what pleasure could he get from them when he didn't know which of the girls was his own and which were the pig and goat in the guise of girls.

Some time later he decided to visit them. When he came to the house of the first girl, the sun had risen long ago, but she was still lazing in bed. Her filthy children were poking about the cottage, chewing crab-apples, acorns and roots.

"That'll be the pig," the father said to himself and went on.

He came to the cottage where the second girl lived. She was just quarrelling with her husband, bleating at him and shaking her head as if she wanted to butt him with her horns. The children were running around the cottage, bleating and baaing. You couldn't hear what you were saying.

"That's the goat," the father thought and went on.

In the evening, he came to the cottage where the third girl lived. She welcomed him, gave him supper, prepared a bed for him. Early in the morning, she got up, washed herself, combed her hair and then woke up the children. She dressed them in clean clothes and gave the family their breakfast. She had a pleasant word for everyone: for her husband, her children, her father and the neighbors, too.

"That is my own daughter," the father said to himself.

Since that time, people have multiplied and nowadays there are women more than enough. This is hardly surprising, considering they have come from three races at once: one human, another piggish and the last, goatish. Just watch them for a while. It isn't hard to discover who comes from which.

The Hell-Hen

There was once a farmer and he was terribly rich. He had two houses, four horses, forests and fields, meadows and moors, a flock of sheep and twenty cows. However he did not have a wife or children and he was quite alone. Everyone knew it was a hell-hen that brought him his wealth. People often saw it disappear down his chimney in the likeness of a fiery chain giving off bright sparks. At such times, they quickly crossed themselves, because they knew that to have a hell-hen meant to have a pact with the devil. They also knew that once a man took in a hell-hen, he couldn't get rid of it that easily. The hell-hen would be with him and near him all the time. It would take possession of his soul, not even allowing him to leave this world until someone else took him as his own.

All the same, as you see, there was a man who chose to have a hell-hen. For a hell-hen our rich farmer really did have, and this tale will tell us all about it.

The farmer had a hen in his yard that was as black as the blackest coal. He once watched and waited while the hen laid an egg and while it was still warm he slipped it under his armpit. For nine days the farmer carried the egg around under his armpit and during those nine days, he neither washed nor combed his hair. After nine days, a chicken hatched out of the egg. What an ugly, scraggy, filthy, little hen it was!

"Welcome, farmer!" squawked the draggletail. "You are mine and I am yours."

"Welcome to you, too, hell-hen!" said the farmer. "Let it be as you say: you are mine and I am yours. In any case, I have no one else in the world."

The hell-hen settled down in the farmer's house. It slept in his pocket and ate with him from the same dish. At night, it would fly here and there and return home through the chimney in the form of a fiery chain.

"What should I bring you, farmer?" it would ask every day.

"Bring me grain," said the farmer. At other times, "Bring me linen for shirts." Or, "Today you can bring me a sheep and a ram."

The hell-hen kept bringing him whatever he asked and the farmer grew richer and richer.

"What should I bring you, farmer?" it asked again one day.

"What could you bring me?" the farmer thought for a while. "The stables are already full of cattle, the barns are full of grain, the clothes chests are full of cloth. But you know what? Bring me money, I could still find some room for some money."

The days and years passed. All the coffers, all the drawers, all the jars, all the jugs, all the pots, all the pans were full of money. But the farmer had no use for it and it gave him no pleasure any more. People avoided him and the servants wouldn't stay. They all knew that his wealth was gained dishonestly and it was best to keep away from it. The farmer's hair had turned white long before, his back was bent, his body was riddled with all kinds of diseases. More and more, he longed to be freed of his cares and pains and to rest where for many years his father and mother had lain. But the hell-hen! The hell-hen never stopped hopping around him and demanding work.

"What should I bring, farmer?"

"Ah, what I need is dung!" groaned the old farmer, whose bones were aching badly just then.

By the morning, the whole house and the whole yard was full of dung, which the hell-hen must have brought from all over the country. The farmer's servants had more work than they could cope with to get rid of that stench.

160

The farmer became more and more obsessed with the idea of getting rid of the hell-hen. But who would take it from him?

He begged his brother, his stepbrother and his brother-in-law, his first cousin, his second cousin and his cousin once removed, his neighbor to the right, his neighbor to the left, but nobody would take the hell-hen from him.

One day a young stranger stopped at his house. Her name was Catherine and she was looking for work.

"I can't take on any more servants," he told her, "the house is full of them already," which was far from the truth.

"But as you've happened to come when I'm feeling much better, I'll give you a gold coin and this hen."

Catherine didn't like the look of the hen, but the ducat was beautiful, so she took both and even thanked him politely. She had hardly reached the road when the hen under her armpit squawked, "You are mine, Catherine, and I am yours!"

"Ah! it's a hell-hen!" the girl exclaimed in fright. She realized at once why she had been given the coin, to take the devil away from the house.

She flung the hen down on the ground and took to her heels. But the hen hopped along beside her, squawking, "You are mine, Catherine, and I am yours."

Catherine stopped and thought quickly, "The only way to get out of this is by a trick."

She went into a store, changed the gold coin and bought a new skirt. She put it on and screwed the old one up under her arm. At that moment, who should appear but a rag-and-bone man, driving his cart.

"Rags and bones, rags and bones!"

"What would you give me for this old skirt?" asked Catherine, adroitly wrapping it up with the hell-hen inside.

"A thimble and two needles, agreed?"

Catherine agreed. As we know very well, she would have given him the skirt for nothing.

The rag-and-bone man drove on, cracking his whip when suddenly

the hell-hen jumped up on the shaft and squawked, "You are mine, Matthew, and I am yours!"

"Goodness me, it's a hell-hen!" the rag-and-bone man shook with fear. He wrapped the hen up in the skirt again and as he was crossing the bridge, he dumped the whole cartful into the river. He whipped the horses so hard that they raced off as if their hooves were on fire. The rag-and-bone man arrived home feeling very pleased with himself for having got rid of the hell-hen so easily. He opened the door of the cottage and almost fainted! There on the bench sat the hell-hen. Seeing him, it squawked, "We did go fast, didn't we, Matthew!"

The rag-and-bone man lost his temper. He seized the filthy hell-hen and thrust it into the hen coop and gave it nothing to eat for two days, not the tiniest little crumb, however much it squawked. On the third day, he took it out of the coop and slipped away with it to the yard belonging to the miller's wife. The miller's wife was just feeding the poultry. The rag-and-bone man pushed the hell-hen through a hole in the fence, and it ran off at once to join the hens, where it pecked and pecked and pecked, because, as we know, it had had nothing to eat for two whole days.

"Go away, you scruffy bird!" the miller's wife chased it away, but the hell-hen took no notice, just stuffing its beak as fast as it could. She caught hold of it by the wing to throw it over the fence. Oh, but that is enough for a hell-hen, if a human does no more than touch it, it already belongs to him.

"You are mine, miller's wife and I am yours!" it squawked.

"So that's the kind of hen you are!" the woman realized at once, but she kept her head. She was an experienced woman of which no one got the better. She carried the hell-hen into the room, put it down on the bench beside the table and said, "If you say you are mine, let it be so. Look, I eat at this table, you will eat on this bench. What do you like to eat best?"

"I like sweet semolina pudding!" squawked the hell-hen.

So during the day the hell-hen sat on the bench and ate sweet semolina pudding. At night, it flew here and there, through the world in the form of a fiery chain and brought the miller's wife whatever she happened to want. Her chests were already full of:

> flour and peas and haricot beans,
> lentils, oats and corn,
> sausages, fat and salted pork,
> beer and brandy, barley wine,
> sheets and linen, eiderdowns,
> wools and silks and velveteen
> and more gold coins than ever you've seen.

Every evening the hell-hen asked, "What should I bring you, mistress?"

The miller's wife told herself the time had come. She now had everything and the only thing she needed was to get rid of the hell-hen. So she said to it, "Dear little hell-hen, fill my loft with wheat."

She secretly made a hole in the loft and the grain trickled through it straight into the mill stream.

The hell-hen ran back and forth with bag after bag of wheat but the wheat kept trickling, trickling through the hole... Sack after sack, night after night... but the loft was never full. Not the devil himself can go on forever. It burnt himself up with strain and exhaustion. The miller's wife found it, claws in the air, all black and charred.

The very same day her gold turned to mould.

A year and a day, her mill was in decay.

Two years went by, she'd but a bucket of rye.

And when another year passed, she had to fast.

"Easy come, easy go," is what people said about the miller's wife's wealth. "Who eats with the devil must have a long spoon."

They say that was the last hell-hen to hatch out in this land. It's probably true. I've never read of one, have you?

Forthcoming from KUSKA HOUSE:

European Fairy Tales

Nineteen of the best known and most typical European fairy tales from nine languages, in new translation.

Beside some famous classics this book contain many new or little known stories like Punished Pride, Prince Bajaja, The Twelve Dancing Princesses, The Twelve Months, The Black Bull of Norroway, Tattercoat, The Firebird, Broad, Tall and Sharp Eyes, Fanta-ghiro and many more. Any reader who enjoys the freshness of the stories in the White Prices, will also enjoy even more stories in the European Fairy Tales. Some are European classics, several centuries old, enjoyed by millions of young and older readers but virtually unknown to the average Canadian or U.S. reader, for whom it would be a very pleasant surprise.

This nice book would be available in plenty of time for Christmas 1988 — ask for it in any better bookstore or write directly to Kuska House, 117 Westmoreland Rd., Kingston, Ontario, Canada, K7L 5C7.

U.S. readers can write to ABC, Cape Vincent, New York 13618-0599. Canadian readers can also order from our exclusive distributor (ABC BOOKS), using one of ABC TOLL FREE numbers:
1-800-267-0949 or 1-800-267-0971 (from area code 613 only).